Reclaimed

To Aurora.

I Love you!.

River Savage xx

RIVER SAVAGE

Reclaimed

©2015

Reclaimed is a work of fiction. All characters, organizations and events portrayed in this novel are either products of the author's imagination or used fictitiously.

All rights reserved. In accordance with the U.S. Copyright Act of 1976, the scanning, uploading and sharing of any part of this book without the permission of the publisher is unlawful piracy and theft of the author's intellectual property. Thank you for your support of the author's rights.

First edition: February 2015

Edited by Becky Johnson, Hot Tree Editing
Cover design ©: Louisa Maggio at LM Creations
Image: stockphoto.com
Formatting by Max Henry at Max Effect
Information address: riversavageauthor@gmail.com

Dedication

To Gilly.

For sharing your story. For inspiring me.
May Max know how beautiful your journey has been.
I love you, friend.

xxx

Note to the Reader

Dear reader,

This is a novella and features the characters from the previous storyline.

The events of *Reclaimed* take place after *Incandescent* and *Affliction*, book one and two in the Knights Rebels MC.

To get the full advantage of the story, and character development, I strongly suggest you read in order.

Happy reading.

River x

Prologue

Nix

"I'M PREGNANT," SHE RUSHES OUT JUST AS I FEEL HER pussy clench around the two fingers I have planted deep inside of her.

"What?" I look up, frozen in the moment as the shock of her words run through me. *I'm pregnant.* My face stills between my wife's legs, her tightness still grips my fingers while her delicious pussy juices cover my mouth and chin. Even in this moment, she's still fucking greedy.

"I'm pregnant," she repeats, but even after the second time she says it, it doesn't fully register. *I'm going to be a dad, again?* I sit back on my legs, totally lost in the news that my wife has my child in her belly. "Are you going to say anything, Nix?" she asks when I don't respond.

"Nix." She tries to pull away, pulling me out of my frozen stare.

"Be quiet." The order comes out as a growl as I slowly move up her body.

"Nix, what—" She starts to complain, but I cut her off when my body covers hers and her eyes come to mine.

"You've got my baby inside of you?" I ask, leaning down into her space. Her eyes search mine, maybe not expecting this reaction from me, but I can't get a hold of it. Knowing she has my child inside of her has my head all over the fucking place.

"Yes," she whispers, her green eyes filling with tears.

"How long have you known?" I question, my mind yelling at me to react calmly, to do something other than interrogate her.

"I found out this morning." A slow smile spreads across her beautiful face, and each time I see it, I fall a little more in love with her.

"You waited all this time to tell me?" I can't soothe the accusation in my voice.

"What's wrong?" She tries to move, but I keep her firmly under me, where I can see her, touch her.

"You have my child inside of you and you fuckin' waited all day to tell me?"

"Yes!" she snaps, rolling to the left to get away from me. Fuck, I'm fucking this up.

"Why the fuck didn't you tell me?" I sit up and watch her carefully. I don't know what the fuck is wrong with me. She's pregnant. Fucking pregnant with my child. My stomach knots in elation, but my head can't get over the fact that she kept quiet all day, rode on the back of my bike today, and tells me while I eat her out, my fingers encased in her heat. *Fuck.*

"I'm telling you now, asshole," she snaps and moves to leave our

2

bed. Her anger excites me, stirs my dick. It's pretty fucking messed up, but that's what I love about this woman; she fucking loves hard, and passionately.

"Where are you going?" I ask, lost in her anger and how it affects me.

"Away from you," she huffs, and even when she's pissed, I know I can make her melt under me. Two minutes, tops.

"Get back here." I pull her back to the bed, positioning her under me.

"You're being an ass," she complains, refusing to make eye contact. She's right. I am, but it's not every day your wife tells you she's carrying your child.

"No, baby. I'm being a man who just found out that his wife was keeping the most fan-fucking-tastic news from him all day."

"I was trying to find the right time," she says to the far wall, and I smirk at her sulking.

"The right time would have been the minute you found out." I take her chin in my fingers and force her to look at me.

"That would have been lame." She rolls her eyes, but I can tell by her reaction, she's caving. "I wanted to do something sweet." She loses her attitude and I know what she needs from me.

"I don't need sweet, baby. I got you." I lean down and take her lips with mine in a soft, gentle kiss.

"Don't use your lines on me, Mr. Knight." She sighs as I move down her body. My head lines up with her belly.

"You got my baby here?" My hands find her belly. A need like no other runs through me, an instinct telling me I need to protect her, protect them. Her hands move to her stomach, one covering mine.

"Yeah, baby. You're gonna be a daddy again." Her voice is thick with emotion and I squeeze my eyes shut. I'm lost in the moment.

Me, naked with my wife, in our bed, now knowin' she carries my unborn child.

"Fuck, I love you, Kadence," I look up at her and watch a tear crawl down her face. "You fuckin' give me light, baby, give me so much fuckin' light I don't know what to do with it. But this," I look down toward her stomach, passing the scars that mar her side, "nothing could ever compare. Nothing. Givin' me somethin', somethin' we made, somethin' of you and me. Fuck, Kadence, I don't know if I want to sink my cock in you and fuck you hard, or hold you and cry." *Fuck, I'm a fucking pussy.*

"Don't cry, babe." Sitting up, she takes my face in her hands.

"You ruined me, woman. Fucking ruined me. I promise you, I'm gonna be the best daddy." I kiss her hard and she takes it all as her tears hit my lips.

"I already know, Nix. If our baby has half the love you show Z, he or she will be blessed." She pulls back to wipe her face.

"If you show half the love you've shown my son, *our* son, then this baby will know nothing but goodness," I counter, 'cause it's the truth. This woman is my fucking light. I'm the luckiest son-of-a-bitch around, and with my child growing in my wife's belly, our family is complete.

1

Nix

ten months later

"KADENCE, DID YOU HEAR ME?" I STOP AT THE THRESHOLD OF our kitchen and watch as my wife stands at the sink. Her long hair sits disheveled on top of her head; knots and frizz hidden by the quick up do. Long gone is the happy, carefree woman who nearly knocked me on my ass with just a smile that afternoon in my son's classroom.

"Huh?" She looks up from the foamy water, her eyes catching mine, but it's like they don't lock. Void of any emotion, as if she's looking straight through me. I have no idea if she even realizes I've been standing here for five minutes.

"I need to go to the club." I repeat my first statement and walk toward her.

"W-what?" She shakes her head out of the fog she seems to have settled into since Harlow was born.

"Shit's goin' down with one of Beau's girls. I have to sort it out," I lie to her, stopping at the counter to give her time to process.

"You can't leave!" Her voice quivers as she drops the cup she's been cleaning for five solid minutes and wipes her hands down the front of one of my old club tees, and her ratty yoga pants. "Harlow will be awake soon, Nix." Her eyes flash with panic and her voice fills with distress. Just like every other time she has panicked with the apprehension of being left alone. I don't know when it began, when our perfectly constructed life started to fall around us, but over the last seven weeks, something has changed. Something I wasn't prepared for.

"You'll be fine, baby. We talked about this," I try to reason with her, but I know no matter what I say, it won't make a difference; it never does. Kadence will freak. She'll break and then she will act like everything is fine. The sooner I get this done, the better.

"Nix, I can't." Her shaky voice almost brings me undone, but I have to stay strong; this is the plan. "You can't leave me alone with her. What if she cries and doesn't…" she trails off, her eyes growing large as she concocts some fucked-up shit in her head. "Oh, God, don't do this to me. I need you. Don't leave me." She walks forward into my space, her hands coming to my leather cut. I see the shake in them before she touches me, can feel the panic in them as she holds me tightly against her. My wife is so fucking lost—lost in her own world of hopelessness. I don't even know how I can help.

"Z is here. You'll be fine." I try to reassure her with the news that she won't be alone entirely. I know Z is only eleven, he should be doing what other kids his age are doing, but leaving him home will make it easier on me, on all of us.

6

"But Z can't help me like you. What if I do something wrong?" Even the way she asks that question has my heart breaking. How could she think she will fuck this up?

Taking her shoulders in my hands, I bend at the waist, get in her face and lock my eyes with hers. "Kadence, I have to go. You've got this, babe. I'll be thirty minutes," I try to encourage her, while watching her reaction carefully. I know this situation is fucked. I've been living it the last seven weeks, but as much as I want to take her in my arms, tell her everything is okay, I can't. I won't tell her that, because it's not. She's not okay. *We're* not okay. The longer I try to step around the issues, the longer it's going to take for her to see that something is wrong. I need my wife back. I need that spark she brings to my gut when she smiles at me. I don't know where or when I lost her, but the Kadence I know doesn't live here anymore.

She looks up at me, disoriented. Her innocent eyes, bewildered, like I'm instructing her on the hardest mission she will ever encounter and it guts me. Where is the woman who took me by the balls and put me in my place? Where is the woman who stood before me, daring me to judge her and her scars? The proud woman I fell in love with is a shell of a woman, and like the coward I am, I don't know if I can bear to look at her anymore.

"Thirty minutes," I repeat, and then lean down, placing my lips to hers. Unlike in the past, when her body would mold into mine and her lips would accept me, I'm met with thin, lifeless lips instead of the softness I once knew. The hardness of her kiss leaves me feeling cold and does nothing to soothe the concern that builds inside of me daily. It does the opposite and proves to me that every one of my concerns are warranted.

"If you loved me, you wouldn't leave me." She holds on to me with a death grip and it's then I realize that if I'm going to leave, I have to do it now.

"But I do, Kadence. I fuckin' love you more than anythin'."

"Then don't leave."

"Admit you need help," I counter, praying she would open up to someone, to anyone.

"Just leave." She pushes at my chest and I feel like a sorry excuse for a husband. A fucking failure who can't even bring his own wife happiness anymore.

"You know I don't want to, but I really have to go," I continue to lie. I don't have any shit going down in the club. In fact, life has been fucking great with the club. If only I could say the same with my marriage.

I have no fucking idea what I'm doing, no idea if I'm helping, or making it worse. The last thing I want to do is push her away, but the woman is already so far gone, I'm planning a search and rescue party as we speak.

"I have my cell." I turn when she doesn't reply and I force myself not to look back into her eyes. I can't let her deter me. I walk out of the kitchen and find Z in the front of the TV.

"You look after our girls, yeah, bud?" I ask, swallowing the sting of deceit of what I'm doing to them all. He pauses his game and turns to face me. His green eyes light up at the task.

"You got it." He puffs out his eleven-year-old chest and a small smile falls on my lips. *Jesus, I love this kid.*

"Love you," I call before I close the door, shutting out his reply. I walk the path to the front drive and mount my Harley.

"Fuck!" I shout out to the quiet street, needing to release my frustration. "Fuck, man, keep it together," I berate myself, knowing I'm doing what I need to do for my wife, for my family.

"You're not leaving her. You're helping," I remind myself, starting the bike up to block out the reply I'm sure to come up with.

Helping her.

If only I knew how to help her.

2

Kadence

"HE LEFT," I WHISPER TO THE EMPTY KITCHEN. I DON'T know if I was expecting a reply, but the heaviness of the truth sits painfully on my chest. Oh, God, he left. Trepidation courses through my body and threatens to overwhelm me, bringing me to my knees as I sink to the floor. I don't understand the uneasiness of my emotions. I don't understand how I can go from riding in a bliss of new baby smell, to feeling like I'm walking blindly in a fog so thick I can't see five inches in front of me.

How could he just leave like this? He knows I can't be left alone. He left when I begged him not to. A prickly sensation of hysteria claws at my heart, squeezing harder and harder until drawing a breath becomes too painful. I can't do this. What if she wakes up? My eyes drift to the cordless phone, sitting on the edge of the kitchen counter. Moving slowly, as my heart pounds in my chest, I crawl over and reach up, snagging it first go. Controlling the small tremble that begins in my hand, I dial the first number that comes from my fingers.

Holly. My best friend.

She will come. She always comes.

"Hello." She answers on the third ring and I can already hear the smile in her voice, but I don't have time to process this new resentment that spreads through me every time I hear her so happy.

"Hey, what are you doing?" I try to come across as composed, but in reality, I'm anything but. My mind and body have been putting on a show for the last few weeks, and I'm tired. So fucking tired, I don't even know how much longer I can keep going.

"I'm just out with Sy," she replies, seemingly oblivious to the mild breakdown I'm having on the floor of my kitchen.

"Doesn't Sy have to get to the club for the club meet?" I question, finding the perfect opening to get her to come over.

"Um, yeah. We're about to head there now." I hear rustling and a muffled voice in the background but can't make out who is talking.

"Well, get Sy to drop you off before," I suggest, keeping the pleading out of my voice.

"We can't. Sy needs to get straight there." She shuts down my suggestion. The panic collars me, causing me to hyperventilate. An invisible force threatens to drag me down into a hole so deep I fear no one can hear my screams for help.

"Holly," I begin as the first sounds of Harlow's whimpers startle me through the crackle of the monitor.

"Oh, is that Low? I'll let you go," she says, and before I can beg for help, she's gone.

Oh, God, what am I going to do now? I let the phone drop to the floor as Harlow's little murmurs turn into cries. Cries that I can't handle.

"Kadence, Low is awake," Z calls out from the living room.

"Yeah, I know, bud. I'll meet you up there," I wheeze out, forcing myself to get it together at least for the kids' sake.

"Hey, baby Low. How you doin'?" I hear Z murmur to his baby sister through the monitor. Her cries stop as she hears her brother's voice, and if I wasn't in total breakdown mode, I would smile at how much she already loves him. If only she loved me like that. If only I could bring that love to her.

I check the clock sitting above the fridge in front of me. It's only been seven minutes. Seven whole minutes. Seven minutes which feel like a lifetime.

"You coming, Kadence?" Z calls again, antsy to play with his sister. We only have one rule, one rule I'm strict on, and that's he can't pick Harlow up out of the crib without me or Nix there. He knows this, so he will be waiting for me to come in for her.

Mindful that the longer I take to get to the kids, the worse it will be for all of us; I gradually pick myself up and force myself to go to my children.

The trek up the carpeted stairs takes longer than normal. The sound of Z's voice and Harlow's cries growing with each step I climb. I stop at the decorated door, a pink plaque hangs in the center; purple letters adorned in golds and pinks spell out her name. Slowly, I drag a long breath through my nose and try to calm myself before I push the door open and force myself to enter.

"Here's momma," Z comforts his sister, his knuckle in her mouth as she tries to suck.

"Hey." I force a smile, knowing if anyone else was here, they would see past my fake bullshit. Not Z, not my sweet Z though.

Moving toward the honey-stained oak crib, I catch the first glimpse of her dark curls. I remember when she was born, the first thing I noticed was her dark hair. Just like her father's. Then she opened her eyes and it was like falling in love in slow motion. Reaching the side of the crib, I peer over and watch as those same eyes come to mine. Green, vibrant and just like her father's. They still melt me each time I see them.

Halting me for a moment, I watch her take everything in around her. These moments, the ones like this, when she looks up at me, her small face recognizing and knowing me, this is what I had envisioned when I thought about becoming a mother, when I grew her in my belly. But these moments are fleeting, barely satisfying me anymore. I love Harlow more than anything, but I'm exhausted. I'm afraid and I feel alone. I'm tired of hiding my despair that I'm not a good mother, or that I'm going to fail her. Even if she does melt my heart, it doesn't stop me from questioning. *Am I enough?* The hopelessness grows day by day, while an unrelenting force keeps pushing me down, lower, deeper and heavier and even on the days I want to fight it, I can't.

"Hey, Low." I smile awkwardly and stand there not understanding how irresolute I had become.

"She seems really hungry," Z prompts, forcing me to bend at the waist, and pick her up from her crib. I keep myself in check, needing to get through the next twenty minutes. *You can't fuck this up when you're her mother,* I remind myself as I place her gently down on the matching oak change table and focus on changing her diaper.

Even this task puts me on edge. Nix has been the one who's been hands on the last seven weeks. I barely know what to do. It's not that I don't want to know, but more I don't know how to want to. If it weren't for the fact I've been trying hard to hide that I'm failing

13

miserably at this mother gig, I would have the sense to ask Nix how he's coping. It's not that I don't care how he is feeling, somewhere deep down inside of me, a small piece is dealing with guilt. Guilt for not caring enough, or for not being happy enough, hell, for not wanting any part of it. I don't know what is happening to me. Spending my days tired, angry and in tears has become my normal. Low is everything I asked for, everything I need. So why does it feel like I have made a mistake?

Holly and my mom voiced their reassurances, suggesting I was just tired. Baby blues is what they called it. But I can't help fear the question I keep asking myself: what if it's more? Was having Harlow a mistake? Did I rush into things when I wasn't ready? The same apprehensions flow through me now just as they have done the past few weeks. I can't pinpoint the moment I realized being a mother wasn't what I was expecting. Yeah, I read the books, searched the forums, but nothing really prepares you for what's to come. No one tells you that having a baby could make you feel so out of control, or lonely. That small, everyday tasks would become insurmountable hurdles. No one tells you, you will spend your days worrying if you're doing everything right, and your nights crying when you fail. But the most heartbreaking thing of all is the numbness. No one told me about the numb feeling, or that it would be the most excruciating pain I would ever experience, even if some days I didn't care.

Shaking my head clear of the thoughts I can't afford to have, I carefully pick up Harlow and sit down in the rocking chair that Nix's father, Red, made for us. When we came home from the hospital with Low, our chair was waiting for us. A note attached telling me Red refurbished the same chair that Nix's mother nursed in.

No one has ever made me a chair before, and the small act of love Red showed me makes me want to sit in the chair every day. But what

I love most about our chair, is the sense of peace it gives me. It's as if I'm chasing peace every second of my day, but when I sit in my rocking chair, the same chair I knew Nix was rocked in, peace never evades me.

"You want to give me fifteen minutes Z, then she's all yours?" I ask Z.

"Sure." He smiles, touching his sister's head once more. "I'll watch some TV." He walks out not waiting for my reply.

"You're not going to give me a hard time are you, Low baby?" I ask, looking down at her as she tries to pull at a stray hair which has fallen from my messy bun. Lifting my shirt, I unclasp my bra and pray to the breastfeeding gods that by some miracle, Harlow has learned how to latch on properly. Resting back, I position her in my arms and before her small pink lips encircle my nipple, the tears begin to fall because I know what's about to happen. I know for the next fifteen minutes, I'll endure the pain of what feeding my child does to me. The stinging will begin as pain shoots through my breast and I won't be able to control the sob that rips from my mouth. I know I will have to resist the need to pull her away, and vow to not feed her anymore. Then the guilt will come, guilt knowing I can't do anything right. I'll try to fight the discontent that weighs heavy on my shoulders. Try to keep the thoughts that this is what she brought into my life away as a small piece of hate eats away at my soul. I fight all these demons alone and broken.

Her small hand will reach up and touch my face, but I'll miss it all, because even if it's the most beautiful thing in the world, I can't stand it. I can't stand the pain and I can't bear to look at my daughter.

I'm a terrible mother.

3

Nix

"HEY, BOSS MAN." JESSE, MY SERGEANT AT ARMS, LOOKS UP from his position, bent over the pool table.

"Hey." I nod, and walk straight to my office.

"What are you doing here?" he calls, but I'm so tightly wound up that I don't stop to answer. Slamming the door shut, I plant my ass in my office chair and let out a shaky breath. Fuck, I shouldn't have left her. My cell vibrates in my pocket, and I pull it out, ready to see Kadence's name flash. Instead, Holly's name comes up.

"Yeah?" I answer, knowing this call is important.

"She called."

I let out a breath I didn't know I was holding and ask what I needed to know. "She sound okay?"

"She didn't sound too bad, but I could hear a little panic. You sure this is a good idea?"

Am I sure? Fuck, I'm not sure of anything these days. "I don't know what else to do, Holly. I've tried talking to her. She just shuts down. She won't go to the doctors. I'm not going to force her, but we can't keep doing everything for her. Besides, Z is there and I trust that she will cope." I believe those words leaving my mouth more than anything. Kadence would never do anything to hurt Low. Her fears and insecurities come from the idea of failing Low or not being the best for her. This fucked-up thinking she has is only amplified by the fact that Low just won't settle.

"You should talk to her, Nix. Tell her what you need from her."

"I've tried, Hol. She won't listen. The only way I can help her is by showing her this isn't normal."

"We both know she's aware it's not normal, Nix."

"Well, if you have a better idea, have at it!" I snap, taking my frustration out on her. I hear Sy in the background, and I know he'll be pissed if I upset his woman. "Sorry, I'm just trying to deal."

"It's okay. You're tired. I'm not just worried about her but about you, too."

"Don't worry about me. Let's just focus on Kadence, yeah?" I ask, not needing a therapy session. I just need my fucking wife back.

"Mom and I are going to come over tomorrow. We can talk to her again then," she says, giving me some small hope.

"Call Kadence's mom. You'll need reinforcements," I add, knowing how bad she was today. Maybe if she hears if from all four of us together, she might listen to what we have to say.

"Right, okay, well, keep me posted," she rushes, ending the conversation. I know she likes to think she has it under control, but

Holly feels as helpless as I do.

"Yeah," I reply before hanging up. I pocket my phone and rest my head on the desk. Jesus, who would have thought ten months ago this is where we would be? Me, hanging in my fucking office, hiding from my wife.

Unease settles in my gut. Feeling disconnected with her burns me, but what eats at me more than anything is knowing she is suffering. Whatever is going on, I just wish we could fucking sort it, move on from it and be a fucking family again.

I fucking miss my wife.

★★★

"How you doin', bud?" I ask Z as I walk through the door a few hours later. After I got off the phone with Holly, I lost myself in some paperwork. During the past seven weeks, I've neglected my duties in the club. Beau, my VP, has had to step up and take on my work while the rest of the boys have been dealing with their own shit: Sy with Inked Me, and Jesse with Liquid.

"Good," Z mumbles, continuing into the kitchen. I follow behind him feeling some tension.

"You okay?" I put my keys and wallet down on the counter and watch him carefully.

"You told her thirty minutes," he snaps, anger dancing in my son's eyes.

He's pissed.

"She okay?" I ask, not certain I want to know the answer.

"She's hiding in the bathroom." He places his dish in the sink, starting to wash it. I don't respond. I just watch him.

If Kadence is in the bathroom, then he's been looking after Low.

"Low okay?" I swallow past the anger and defeat that begins to

18

grow. I hate this, fucking hate it for Z and Low, but hate it more for Kadence.

"I rocked her 'til she fell asleep."

"You're a good big brother, Z." I give him a smile. He doesn't smile back; instead, he looks so confused.

"What's happening, Dad?" he asks straight to the point, looking as unsure as I feel. I step forward and wrap my arms around him. Fuck, when did he get so grown up?

"We got some shit to get through, bud, but we're gonna get there. Know that we are gonna fix it." I kiss the top of his head.

"Is it something that I did?" his small voice asks. And the young man who just called me out for taking longer than I should have, seems so small; worried he's done something to cause the darkness in our home.

"Bud, this isn't about you. I promise. This is somethin' that Kadence and I need to work through."

"But I don't want you to get a divorce." His arms squeeze me on the last word. Fuck me. *Divorce?*

"Hey." I pull back, looking him straight in his eyes. "That's not ever gonna happen, Z. I promise you. Sometimes it takes a while to adjust with a new baby. You have nothin' to worry about, okay?" I hold his gaze, needing him to understand this isn't about him. He slowly nods in my arms as I hold him a little longer before I step back.

"You okay?" I ask, watching him wipe his eyes. It's moments like this, I want to shake her, show her what she is missing. The Kadence I knew would rather die than hurt our son, but now, he's standing in front of me trying to hold his shit together and she wouldn't give one fuck.

"Yeah, I'm gonna go play Xbox." He walks out and I give myself a moment to cool down. Fuck. I knew things were bad, knew I was losing control, but I thought I was protecting Z from it. I was clearly fucking wrong.

After calming myself, I take the steps two at a time and go to find my wife. I'm at the end of my rope. Something has got to fucking give, something to get her to realize that what is happening can no longer go on.

"Kadence?" I knock on the bathroom door and wait for her to answer. "Kadence," I call again when she doesn't respond. I know when she is stressed, when things become too much for her, she likes to hide in here. The first time she checked out, I found her sitting in the empty tub, staring vacantly ahead. I didn't know what the fuck was happening. I walked in late one day with Low screaming in her crib, a confused Z by her side trying to keep her calm, and Kadence sitting in an empty shower, ignoring us all. It took me thirty minutes for her to come back, but it was like a piece of her was missing

"Kadence, just fuckin' respond." I knock again, that small unease in my gut twitches, and something unsettling has my next knock turning into a bang when my arm reaches up again. She doesn't respond and the dread that forms in the pit of my gut twists into something that I wasn't prepared for.

"Open this fuckin' door before I knock it down." My fear comes out as anger, but each second she doesn't respond, is another second that my doubt takes over. I step back, lift my leg, and in one forceful kick, I break past the lock; the door flying back in a loud thud. My eyes scan the bathroom in frantic need to know she is safe, that she hasn't done something stupid, something I would never forgive her for. My body convulses when I see her sitting on the shower floor.

Her head comes up, surprise written all over her face as if my entry into the bathroom is a shock. I can see she has been crying, but the despair and anger ripping through my body doesn't let me register what she needs. I'm too pissed off.

"What the fuck is your problem?" I spit out, watching her body recoil from my words.

She recovers, but doesn't respond, just looks at me so devoid of anything which only causes my anger to grow. Stepping forward, I pull the glass shower door open while she continues to look straight through me. My first instinct is to pick her up and shake some life back into her, but I know she's so far in her head right now, it won't get me anywhere. Instead, my hand goes to the tap, not bothering to warm the water, and I let it rush over her. Her gasp fills the small glass enclosed area right before she moves to escape, but I react quicker, holding my frame in the door way.

"Fuckin' talk to me, dammit!" I shout and she trembles under my stare.

"Where the fuck were you?" She finally reacts, trying to push me out of the way. "You left. You said thirty minutes, Nix." Her fists connect with my chest and her voice cracks as she begins to sob.

My arms come around her, pulling her wet body into mine, holding her while she screams out and comes undone. I fucked up. I know I did, but I can't help feel a small glimmer of hope grow in me that she's finally reacting. I hold her for a brief moment, the water still falling over her back, splashing both of us. I reach back and shut it off, holding her firmly in my arms.

"Just breathe, baby." I reach for the towel and wrap her tightly in it. Silent sobs rack her body. "Deep breaths," I encourage again, when I sense her losing the battle to control them. I fucking hate myself knowing I did this to her, but I don't know how much more of it I can handle. It takes her a few more minutes before her breathing slows and her sobs finally fade.

I don't move her, afraid to set off another round, so I hold her in my arms, praying I haven't just fucked up shit even more. Hoping that eventually she will talk, because somewhere deep down inside of me, I have that sinking feeling. The one that tells me if things don't change, I don't know how much longer I'll have her for. And not having Kadence in my life, is not an option.

It will *never* be a fucking option.

4

Kadence

I SIT ON THE SIDE OF THE BATHTUB AS NIX DRIES ME OFF.
My clothes stick to my body and my hair hangs over my face. I don't
say anything. I can't even look at him let alone talk to him. *How could
he just leave me?*

After I fed Low, Z came up and played with her a little while I sat
and watched them. I can't pinpoint exactly what it was that set me
off. Low was being fussy, as usual. Z was asking questions and as the
time ticked over, Nix was getting later and later. It all became too
much—my unease rose inside of me with each minute that passed.
The pressure of when, or *if* he was even coming home at all amplified
the panic that lay dormant in me.

"Baby?" Nix calls, pulling me from my thoughts. I used to like it when he called me baby, when he would touch me, make me feel beautiful, but now somewhere in my mind, the word *baby* doesn't represent what it once did. His touch doesn't soothe me like it used to, and not one part of me feels beautiful.

"What?" I shrug him off, not wanting his hands on me as I slide down from where he placed me.

"We need to talk about what happened." He follows me into our bedroom, clearly looking for a fight. He does this all the time, pushing me deliberately until he gets the reaction he wants. It's in those moments I feel like he is judging me.

"I'm really tired. I'm going to bed." I turn and pull out sweats and one of Nix's old club tees from my dresser.

"No, we are gonna talk now." I ignore him, not in the mood for this tonight. Moving to walk past him, his hand comes out, wrapping around my bicep.

"Get the fuck off me," I hiss, pulling out of his hold as he reels back at my tone.

"Kadence." He moves in but my hand comes up.

"You touch me again and I'm out. I'm not even kidding, Nix. I will pack a bag so goddamn fast you won't even see it coming," I threaten. My head is all over the place, my mind in a constant battle with itself. Fuck, how did it get like this?

"What the hell, Kadence?"

"I can't handle you being late," I shout, pointing to the broken bathroom door. All of my insecurities, feelings of being hopeless, fears of failing, surface to the top as my anger flows through me. "I fucking lost it tonight because of you not coming home when you said you would!"

"Dad?" Z calls through the door, halting whatever was about to go down between us.

"Go," I whisper, afraid of what Z's already heard. Knowing our son waits on the other side of the door alone has Nix looking torn. His eyes pleading with me for something I can't give him.

"Yeah, coming, bud," he calls out as I walk past him. I don't give him another chance to try to talk to me; instead, I head back into the bathroom. *My safe place.*

"This conversation isn't over. We *will* talk about this, Kadence," he warns, but I don't respond. What is there to say? He left, came home, and found me at my worst. It wasn't the first time it's happened.

I hear the bedroom door open and then shut. I let out an unsteady breath I didn't know I was holding. Peeling myself out of my wet clothes, I re-dress and rush through my bedtime routine. It's not yet dinner time, but the reality of the day is too much for my state. I know Nix must be worried, coming home to see me like this, but sometimes just stepping away when the darkness starts to consume me helps.

Confining myself within the marble walls of my bathroom gives me a disturbing comfort. I find solace in the silence. If that doesn't work, then my screams block out her cries, reminding me I still have a voice when I release a small piece of my fear.

Letting the sound of my pain echo off the walls gives me the reprieve I am searching for. Does it fix the issue that something is happening with me? No. Nor does it make Harlow stop crying and give me the peace my mind so desperately needs in order to heal. No. Sitting in the shower, locked away in the bathroom, hiding from my family is the only way I can deal. I can block out everything around me and be someone else. Somewhere else. I'm not a mom who is laced with guilt for not being happy when I have everything to be happy for. I'm not this panicky person whose heart races just from picking out what clothes Low is going to wear. Pretending is my relief. It's how I manage to block it all out. I know it isn't healthy, but some days pretending is just easier.

After brushing my teeth, I climb into bed and bury myself under the covers. I know I should go out, check on Low and Z, but now that Nix is home, I know he will have it under control. With the day's exhaustion catching up on me, I force my eyes shut, and pray I fall asleep before Nix comes back. The last thing I need tonight is to go over what happened today.

★★★

"Kadence?" I hear whispered into my ear. I open my eyes and find the room is shadowed in darkness as Nix's bedside lamp illuminates his side of the room. I must have fallen asleep.

"Don't touch me." I pull away, hiding myself further under the covers. This is something I have allowed the last few weeks, him holding me in the quietness of our bed. But tonight, I can't even stand to have him near me.

"I don't want to fight, baby. I don't even want to talk. Just let me hold you."

"Nix." I tense when he pulls me closer to him. "Not now." I keep my eyes closed, needing to find sleep again.

"Fuckin' when then?" He pulls away, hitting the empty space of the bed beside him.

"Just don't touch me," I repeat, sinking further into my cocoon of bed covers.

"Jesus, Kadence. The only fuckin' time I touch you is in my sleep. Don't fuckin' take that from me too. Don't push me away when I'm hangin' on by a fuckin' thread. I miss you, baby. I miss your hands,

26

your smile. Fuck, I miss your face."

"I'm not trying to push you away, Nix, but you need to give me more time." I keep my eyes closed. Too afraid to turn and see what his eyes are telling me.

"This is not just about you, Kadence. There are two people in this marriage. How long do I have to wait? How long until we come undone?"

I turn, pissed off he just won't give up. "You're unbelievable, do you know that? You don't get sex for seven weeks and you're threatening me with this bullshit? You want to fuck? Huh? You want to take me when it's clear that I don't want it? You want me to just lay there and fucking pretend?"

"What the fuck is wrong with you, woman? You think this is about sex? You don't talk to me. You won't let me hold you and you won't tell me what is happening with you. When was the last time you went outside? The last time you laughed, or even smiled? " He continues to throw everything I'm failing at right back at me, and each jab makes me hate myself even more.

"I'm just tired, Nix. Last time I checked, I just had a baby. A baby who won't eat, and who has ruined my fucking body. Who screams for twenty-hours a day. And you want to know what the fuck is wrong with me?" My insecurities surge forward as I scream at the top of my lungs. Fear, hatred, and pain fuel my rage, yet a small part of me knows he has a right to be worried. It's not just about Harlow and what is happening with her. It's about us and me, because something is happening with *me*.

"Don't put words in my fuckin' mouth, woman." He runs his hand through his hair in frustration. I can't do anything to fix this. To fix me. We both sit in silence looking at each other.

Broken.

Falling apart.

"I don't know what you want from me," I whisper. Communication was never this hard. The distance growing further between us as each day passes makes me afraid that this is what we've become.

"I just want to bring you happiness, baby," he sighs, but before I can tell him I don't think he can, Harlow's cries come through the monitor. I move off the bed to go to her, knowing she will need to be fed.

"You walk out of this room, Kadence, you walk out on me." His cold tone stops me from moving any further. It's the same tone he used in the bathroom. "Leave her," he commands, but the thought of continuing this conversation, where we tear each other down, has me fighting him.

"Nix, I have to check on her." I continue to the door.

"Don't you dare leave this fuckin' room. I'm important too. I'm your fuckin' husband. Do you hear me? *We* are important." His hand sweeps across his nightstand, causing one big crash that sends everything tumbling to the floor. I'm frozen in place, my hand resting on the door handle. The room is silent. The shock of what has gone on tonight so raw I don't think either of us knows how to process it.

"I don't know what you want from me," I repeat, closing my eyes when Harlow's cries grow louder, sending my anxiety rising. Doesn't he know he's only making it worse?

"Jesus, I don't know. Give me a look, smile at me…fuckin' touch me. Give me a connection that says we're on the same fuckin' side. I can't continue to stay in this place we are in. I'm drowning here, Kadence. We both are, and I just don't know if I can keep treading water for both of us. You have to help me, baby. You have to want us to survive." He falls to the bed, his head dropping to his hands. Seeing him like this, in this state makes me realize that our situation is bigger than me, than him. It's bigger than either one of us realize.

"That's not fair." I release the handle and turn, collapsing against the wall. The wind knocks out of me as his words resonate within me. We *are* drowning and I have to stop fighting. At this realization, my knees become weak. Standing becomes too hard. I slide down the wall, dropping my ass to the carpet.

"Life isn't fair, Kadence. I wish it was, but it just isn't. Look where we both have come from; look where life has taken us. We won't survive if you won't talk to me, Kadence. Talk to someone." He stands to come to me, but having him in my space only makes things worse.

"Please don't." I draw in a breath, defeated. His frustration and concerns only prove what a bad mother I've been, what a bad wife I've become.

"Don't what, Kadence? Don't make me walk away. I want my wife back. I don't know what's happened, but I don't like who you've become." His voice is pained, as broken as my soul feels. His confession doesn't surprise me, but it still burns. I know *I* don't like who I've become. How do I expect Nix to like me?

"You don't think I ask myself that question every day? That I don't look at myself and ask what is wrong with me? I don't know who I've become, Nix. All I know is I should. I should know who I am." My head thuds against the wall in defeat. I can't keep going on like this. I can hear Harlow's cries quietening, as she resettles herself, but that doesn't stop me from wanting out of this room.

"I know who you are, Kadence. You're the woman I love. The most amazin' mother to our daughter, our son." Saying Z is my son pulls at me harder. The fact that he, too, is affected by what is happening hurts even more. Nix walks over and squats to my level, careful not to get into my space, but close enough for me to reach out and touch him if I wanted to.

"Why don't I know that? I should know that Nix."

"You don't have to know. I know, the kids know and that's enough."

"It's not enough for me." My hand itches to touch him, to feel his hardness under my fingers, but sitting broken on the floor of our bedroom, I know I can't. I can't touch the man who means everything to me and I hate myself for it.

"When did you stop trustin' yourself?"

"I don't know. When did I stop being myself?" I counter, and my admission halts him for a moment. He crawls forward, coming closer into my space. His warmth, his calming presence wraps itself all over me.

"The first step is askin' for help, baby. Let me help you. You don't have to be alone. Let me learn to breathe the ugliness you see. Let me share the darkness, Kadence. Just don't push me away." His pleading pulls at me, pulls at the hatred that has settled inside.

"I'm not doing good, Nix," I say, looking up and giving him what he needs. What *I* need. "Somewhere along the way, I woke completely lost and overwhelmed. And every day, it gets harder and harder to deal." A sob tears from deep within me, and walls I've been hiding behind crumble down.

"I know, baby." He pulls me into the hardness of his chest. "We're gonna be okay," he promises, and everything in me wants to believe him. Everything in me wants to trust he has me. That he has us. But the truth is, I've drowned in so much self-doubt and uneasiness, that trust seems so far away.

5

Nix

four months later

"YOU STILL HERE?" JESSE WALKS IN, DROPPING HIS KEYS ON the clubhouse bar.

"Yeah, you sort that shit out with Liquid?" I ask. He was called away an hour ago with some staffing issues, leaving the rest of my brothers to sit around and shoot the shit.

"Yeah, we're down a waitress. Need to put another on." Jessie takes a seat next to Brooks, taking a pull from his beer. "You still sitting around talking about fucking babies?" He motions to Harlow, sitting on my lap, and Sy who's down on the floor with his new son, Xzavier, sleeping on his chest.

"Fuck off. You're just jealous," Sy murmurs, running his thumb along baby X's forehead. X, is only six weeks old, but Sy has settled into fatherhood with such ease, anyone would think he'd done it before.

"Jealous? Fuck that. I'm happy where I'm at, asshole," Jesse scoffs, but something in his tone tells me he is full of it. Jesse is the least family orientated man I've ever met. He's loyal, passionate, but talk about settling down, he's out of there.

"Keep telling yourself that, Jesse." I laugh as Harlow reaches for my hand, wrapping her small fist around my finger as she tries to lift it to her mouth. Her mouth opens, and drool pools at the side, showing the first signs of teeth coming through.

"Where are the girls anyway?" Jesse asks, ignoring my jab.

"Girls' day," Sy answers, sitting up when X gets restless.

"They're almost done, so we should head out." I motion to the clock above the bar. The girls are out for some beauty day that Holly and Kadence started doing in Holly's last few weeks of pregnancy. Once every couple of weeks, the girls go out for an afternoon and do their girly shit, spend a fuck-load of money. Doesn't bother me as long as it helps my woman. It gives her some breathing time which means when she's home, she's relaxed.

"How's Kadence doing?" Jesse turns serious. I know what he's asking and I know he's only asking as her friend, but it's not something I like to talk about. But my brothers are my family. They've been through everything with me and stood by my side. Even when I wanted to fucking lock my family up in my home and deal with it by ourselves, they stood by me; never pushing, never giving me a hard time 'cause I wasn't around the clubhouse much. As much as Kadence was pushing me out, I was pushing them out.

When we brought Harlow home, I never knew we would end up where we did. When Addison had Z, it seemed so easy. Z was a good baby; sleeping through the night and even feeding well. The first few weeks of Harlow being home, I knew something was up. The house was unsettled and filled with tension; it all built up until it boiled over. The sleep deprivation didn't help us either. At first, the doctors said it was hormonal, and Harlow was just a fussy baby, but as each week passed, I knew it was more than that. Between the feeding problems, and Kadence's insecurities, she let it build a wall around her, dividing us. The pressure of being a good mom, of not failing, it all became too much for her. I could see it, my brothers could see it, and Z could see it. She wasn't herself until we reached our breaking point; the night I walked through the door and had to reassure Z we weren't falling apart.

It wasn't my intention to push her that night, but maybe deep down I knew that was what was needed. Whatever my reasoning, it worked. The moment she admitted she knew something was wrong, I knew we would be okay. It took a few days, but after talking with her mom, Kadence agreed to book an appointment with her doctor. I don't know what I was expecting when we went, but after discussing our options, we decided that therapy and medication would be our plan of attack. Four months, many tears, and a whole heap of frustration later, things have gradually improved.

Harlow has settled so much these past weeks. She has become calmer and more at peace. Since the tests the Doctors ran on her, we found out she was allergic to milk. Fucking go figure. Her reflux was a result of her hypersensitivity. Kadence's insecurities of not being able to bond with Harlow through breastfeeding set us back a little, but after talking to a few moms and realizing the stress on her would be too much if she took on the diet to continue feeding, she was able to move past it.

We all have.

I'm not saying the last four months have been easy. They haven't. It wasn't as if those pills the doctor had prescribed Kadence fixed everything. We still had our bumps. Lack of sleep was still an issue. Z still had school, and club business was still important. But things became manageable.

"She's doing good, better." I stand and hand Harlow to Beau as I gather up her toys. He takes her easily, lifting her up in the air to make her squeal.

"You ready to get going, bud?" I call out to Z as he walks out of the kitchen.

"Yep," he answers with a mouthful of food.

"Can you take your sister's shit out to the car for me?" I point to the baby bag sitting on the table. He nods and does as I ask, waving to the boys as he goes.

"How you doin'?" Beau asks, knowing I don't want to talk about it, but asking anyway.

"I'm good. We're getting there." I nod, believing it. While we're not back to where we were before Low, we're gradually finding ourselves. "Havin' a family dinner this weekend. I want you all there." I turn back to look at Jesse in particular. The last few weeks Jesse has been missing around here. His family have been giving him a hard time the last few months, and since then, he's been somewhat withdrawn. "First time she's been ready to have you all over at once. I know we've had a fucked-up time the last few months, that's been on her mind. I don't want it to be an issue, okay?" My brothers all nod, knowing this is a good sign.

"I'm there if she's making her lasagna." Jesse smirks.

"You're there even if she's makin' fuckin' eggs," I warn. His brows rise, but he doesn't say anything else.

"But she's making her lasagna though, right?" Hunter, our newest brother calls from behind the bar.

"Yeah." I turn and watch a shit-eating grin spread across his face.

Yeah my woman can cook a mean fucking lasagna. My phone beeps in my pocket letting me know I have a text. Pulling it out, I see Kadence's name flash across the screen.

KADENCE: READY, BABY.

A small smile plays on my lips and I try to ignore the pansy-ass feeling that stirs in my gut at seeing her call me baby. The last four months have been focused on getting Kadence back to a place where she is happy and healthy. But along the way, I've also been hurting. I've been missing the woman I fell in love with. Underneath the broken woman who would stare back, was the woman I needed. I just had to take a back seat until she returned.

NIX: ON OUR WAY. LOVE YOU.

I send the message and look up, catching Brooks watching me. Brooks is close to a big brother, always giving me advice, my voice of reason when I'm losing my shit.

"You okay?" he asks. He picks up on everything, always watching everyone.

"Yeah, girls are ready," I say, nodding to Sy. He lifts his chin and stands, ready to head out and get Holly.

"Thank fuck. This daddy-daycare bullshit you've got going on here is ruining my mood," Jesse snarks, before snatching Low from Beau's arms. He talks shit like this all the time. Says having Low and X here is a pain in his ass, but we all know he secretly loves it.

He lays Low down on his lap, tickling her belly until her high-pitch squeal escapes her little mouth. The one she only does for her uncle Jesse. *Fucker.*

"To do that, I need my kid, asshole," I retort, waiting for him to get his fill.

"You're so fuckin' full of it, Jesse." Sy calls him out, picking up X's baby bag and shaking his head. Jesse ignores both of us as he continues to blow raspberries on her belly.

Just watching the scene, I find myself chuckling at how Low already has fucking bikers wrapped around her little finger. *Fuck, we have turned into a daddy daycare.*

"Quit fuckin' around, Jesse. I wanna go see my wife," I snap, watching the clock and knowing I should be on the road.

"Fine, but when are you going to let me babysit her?"

"Fuckin' never," I respond, taking her from him and the boys all snort.

"Why the fuck not?" He sounds offended, but I've no idea why. The fucker can't take anything seriously.

"'Cause I'll come home and you'd probably be fuckin' some bitch on my couch while she's having a nap." I laugh as I see his eyes glaze over.

"Fuck off." He shakes his head, clearing whatever was running through his mind. "Laugh all you like, but one day you will need me, and I'll fucking remember this."

"Don't hold your breath, Uncle Jesse." I shake my head, walking to the bar to get one of Harlow's bottles. "Don't forget, dinner next Saturday night, seven. Don't be late," I remind them without a backward glance as I head out to my truck.

After buckling Low in, we drive out of the compound with Sy following. Five minutes later, we pull onto Main Street, a few blocks away from the spa the girls spent the afternoon.

"You okay, bud?" I ask Z when I realize how quiet he's been on the drive over.

"I'm good, Dad." He looks up and gives me a grin, and I relax. After all the shit with his mom and the stress over Kadence, I've been worried. But with the help of Kadence's parents and Red, we've been able to keep him feeling all the love around him.

"Thanks for helping me out today with Low."

"Not that I did anything, anyway. Jesse and Beau just hog her the whole time," he complains, and I chuckle at how true that is. The kid is pissed that he has to share his sister. But he's right. Jesse and Beau are taken with her. If Sy let anyone touch X, they could share, but that fucker has a lock on him that no one is touching. Except when Holly is around to tell him to pull his head out of his ass.

"Get used to it, bud. She is kind of cute." I smile as we pull up at the spa where the girls are waiting out front. Once we come to a complete stop, Z jumps out of the front seat as Kadence waves goodbye to Holly and walks to the passenger side.

"Hey, Mom." Z throws his arms around Kadence.

"Hey, bud. How are you?" She kisses the top of his head as she looks up at me and smiles, one of her fucking amazing smiles. Z started calling her mom around the time things got heavy. He never asked and we've never talked about it. I've given him plenty of opportunities to open about it, but he won't. It's something we will keep an eye on, but at this point, we aren't concerned. He seems grounded, happy.

"Did you have a good time?" Z asks, letting go and moving to the back seat. Kadence holds the door open for Z, before leaning in and kissing Low on the forehead.

"Hey, Low baby," she whispers before closing the door and moving back to the front. I keep my eyes trained on her waiting for her answer.

"Yeah, we did." She smiles and climbs up into the truck.

"Did you guys have fun?"

"Jesse and Beau hogged Low." Z tattles on his uncles, pulling a laugh from Kadence. The sound causes me to close my eyes and savor the joy in it.

"You know your sister has them wrapped around her little finger." She reminds him of what I've already said.

"Yeah, yeah. But she's *my* sister." He reaches over and touches her head. Harlow giggles at the contact from her brother.

"How was your day, baby?" she asks, but instead of answering, I lean over and wait for her to lean in the rest of the way and give me her lips.

She gets the hint, her lips finding mine in a light kiss. Before I can take the kiss deeper, Z interrupts. "Ewww, get a room," he complains, halting our kiss.

Kadence smiles against me, but I'm not about to let my eleven-year-old tell me what to do.

"Later," Kadence whispers when I don't move and my brows find my hairline.

"Yeah?" I ask as she sits back and buckles herself in. She looks up, a small blush finding her cheeks. If she's saying what I think she is saying, then my straining cock is in for a fucking good surprise tonight. Last time I touched Kadence, hell, saw her fucking naked was when she was pregnant with Low. I close my eyes and try to keep my raging emotions in check.

"Let's go, Dad. Come on," Z says from the back seat, oblivious to what is happening in the front.

"Day was good. You have a good day with Holly?" I ignore Z and put the truck in reverse.

"I did, thank you, baby." She rests her head back, moaning

slightly. The sound going straight to my dick, excited at being woken from its hibernation. It's been a long time, and hearing that sound come from her lips does things to my cock that I have no idea how to contain. It's something Kadence and I need to talk about, just not right now. So instead of feeding her some line about her being relaxed and what her moan does to me, I take my family home, ready for an early night.

★★★

"She okay?" I look up from the TV when Kadence comes in from putting Harlow down later that night.

"Yeah, she's asleep. Hopefully settled for the night." She climbs into bed, pulling the blanket up to her waist.

I flick the show off, and roll over to face her.

"You okay?" I ask, needing to know where she's at. She doesn't like it when I ask too many times, so I check in with her at least once a week. Something that I won't budge on. Even if she gives me attitude about it.

"I'm okay. Doing really good." She smiles and I don't doubt her for one second. I can see the truth reflected in her eyes.

"I love you." I pull her closer to me.

"I love you, too."

"I've missed you." I move my lips down to hers and pray she doesn't tense—something that has been a normal occurrence these last few months. She sinks into me and my body lets out a soft sigh. I move my lips from her mouth, slowly working down her neck.

"Hmm," she murmurs as I lightly nip at her throat. Inside, I'm high fiving myself. My cock strains in my boxers, standing to attention, ready for some affection. My hand moves to her stomach, finding an exposed piece of skin between her pajama top and bottoms. Her head rolls to the side as my mouth sucks a little harder. Fuck, this is what my body has been craving for so fucking long. Slowly, I slide my hand up her side, lost in the softness of her skin. It's been too fuckin' long, I hate that I can't remember the feel of her tits in my hands. My thumb grazes the swell of her breast, but at my touch, she tenses.

"Is this okay?" My head comes up, praying she doesn't pull away.

"Yeah, I think so." She nods carefully, giving me the go-ahead. My heart is racing and my hands are shaking. I feel like a teenager, eager and fumbling. My hand moves back to her breast and on contact, she tenses again. Only this time my confidence takes a blow.

"I'm sorry. Don't stop." She sighs when I move off her.

"You're not ready." I try to keep the disappointment out of my voice, but I know I fail.

"I am. I want to so badly. I don't know what's wrong with me." She shakes her head and I feel her frustration; my cock feels her frustration.

"I know things have been all over the place, Kadence, but I don't want to push you. I miss you, and as much as I need to sink my cock inside you, I'm not gonna do it while you tense at my touch."

"I miss you, too." She sits up beside me. "I'm just nervous."

"You don't need to be nervous, baby. You have nothing to be worried about."

"That's okay for you to say, Nix. Your body hasn't changed. I'm not the same person I was before Low and neither is my body."

"No, Kadence. You're not. And I wouldn't expect you to be the same person after our year. But do you think that bothers me?"

"Come on, Nix. Don't tell me you enjoy this Kadence? The one afraid of fucking up, of failing again." She pulls the blankets up and I know I've lost her tonight.

"I'm not going to lie. Not being able to touch you, be with you, has been fuckin' hard. I'm horny as fuck, but this is all about you. I'm followin' your lead, baby. You tell me what you need. I'll give it to you. I'll be there for you."

She looks apprehensive, as if the thought of being truthful will only make the situation worse.

"Always truth, baby. Tell me what you need."

"Okay, I want to. I want that connection. I just need to be in control. I know what I'm asking is a big deal. Something that you might not be able to give me, but this is what I need. I don't want to lose you, Nix, and I know I'm asking so much after everything we've been through, but please, don't pull away."

"Pull away? Why the fuck would I pull away now?" I shift and hold her gaze. I don't know what else I have to do to prove to this woman that nothing she can do would push me away.

She doesn't say anything and I can see her fighting her insecurities. It guts me she feels like this. Does she not know how fucking amazing she is? How her body, even after the fire, after having Low, is the most rocking body I've ever fucking seen? And it's mine. All fucking mine.

"Men need sex, Nix. I know that." She shrugs, her gaze looking down at her hands now resting in her lap.

"Kadence," I sigh, not sure how I can even begin. "I fuckin' love you. Yes, your pussy is fuckin' incredible, but, baby, you're more than that to me." She huffs, not liking my reply to her stupid-ass assessment of what I need. I reach over to the lamp on my nightstand and flick the switch to off.

"What are you doing?" she asks as I lay back down, tucking her back into my front.

"I'm not talkin' about this anymore. We're not fuckin'. I'm gonna hold you and we're gonna sleep. And maybe tomorrow we'll try again."

"But I wanna try tonight."

"You're not ready, baby, and I'm not fuckin' pushin' it."

"Nix."

"Just got you back, Kadence. My cock can wait. I don't think I can cope if you check out like that again," I admit, hating the fear in my confession. I know we've moved past that part of our life, but the thought of going back to that place has me on edge. "Just know, baby, I'm always gonna be here. I love you and when you're ready, I'm gonna sink my cock home, doin' it knowin' you fuckin' want it as much as I do."

"But—" she begins, but I'm not budging on this. I'm done.

"Just leave it alone, Kadence. Just give me your mouth and I'll get my fill."

"I love you, you know?" She doesn't give me her mouth, needing the last say.

"I know, baby, and I fuckin' love you." She moves in, and brings her lips to mine. Her tongue makes the first move, skimming along my lips, seeking entry. I let her push into my mouth, giving her full control like she asked. I might not like handing it over, but I will if that's what she needs. I push all thoughts of sex out of my head, and let Kadence's kiss take over. I allow her mouth to tease me into submission while her taste tempts me to lose control. I had forgotten how well my woman can kiss, to the point that I nearly come undone.

Yeah, this waiting business is gonna be fucking hard.

6

Kadence

"HE'S BEEN WAKING UP ONCE A NIGHT FOR THE LAST week." Holly tells my mom the next morning as we sit around watching Harlow sit up on her own and Xzavier try to roll over.

Last night after Nix and I talked, we kissed like teenagers for what felt like hours, before finally drifting off to sleep. I don't know why, but the whole scene felt more erotic; knowing that we both wanted it, but holding off and making out like horny teenagers.

"Wow, that is amazing," I smile, ignoring the slight pang of jealousy that Holly has had a breeze with baby X. I know everyone is different, and with Low's allergy, things would always be harder, but that small wish that I had what she has, stirs in me. Holly is everything I'm not in a mother. Where I stress, she's easygoing. When I freak out, she's calm. It's one of those things that even I can see the irony in, but I'm truly happy for her. I'd never wish what Nix and I went through with Low on anyone. It's just sometimes hard when I hear how easy it could have been. I have to remind myself that every baby is different. Every journey is different, and it doesn't make it worth more or less. It just is what it is.

I've come a long way in the last four months. The despair and feeling worthless is no longer there. Some days are still hard. Harlow's allergy isn't something that will just go away, and we deal with it constantly. But at least I feel like I have a handle on it. That day, four months ago, was my rock bottom. Hearing Nix admit that he couldn't do it anymore was the wake-up call I needed. I knew I was drowning, but I didn't want to acknowledge that I needed help. I wanted the happy family, the perfect child, and I had that, but it wasn't what I had expected. I felt weak, but admitting failure was not an option. Looking back now, I know I wasn't failing as a mother, but when every day becomes a fight against the current, you lose the energy to swim. Dealing with postpartum depression didn't make me less of a mom, it was a symptom of motherhood. I didn't plan for it, but I sure learnt from it. In all honesty, I still am.

"You okay, darling?" Mom asks, pulling me from my place of reflection.

"Yeah." I smile, shaking away the fog. Holly looks me over. Concern fills her eyes, but she has nothing to be worried about. I'm finally in a good place.

"So, X is going to his first sleepover at Mom and Dad's next weekend," Holly continues, taking the focus off me like the good best friend she is.

"He is?" I ask as a small sliver of panic runs through at the thought of leaving Low for a night.

"Yeah, Sy has organized this amazing night away for Valentine's Day. I can't wait. What are you and Nix doing?"

"I don't know." I look to my mom, wondering if Nix has spoken with her. She doesn't give anything away, shaking her head. "We haven't discussed it." I shrug, wondering if Nix has even thought about it.

"I'm sure he will plan something nice." My mom's gentle smile warms me.

"We'll see." I brush it off, not holding my breath. Nix can't even touch me without me freaking out. Something I haven't shared with my mom or Holly yet. I highly doubt he will organize anything romantic.

"So, do you need to go shopping?" I ask Holly, eager to change the subject.

"Yes." She lights up at the idea of shopping. "Let's go Tuesday, after playgroup."

I nod, agreeing to a shopping spree. "You never know, you might need something for yourself." She winks but I don't respond. Like I said, I won't hold my breath.

★★★

"Nix! How many times do I have to tell you to quit leaving your shit on the floor," I yell out from our bedroom four nights later.

"What's wrong, baby?" Nix walks in wearing a towel. His dark hair is slick with water from his shower.

"Don't fucking *baby* me," I snap, not giving a damn that I know I'm in a shitty mood and clearly looking for a fight. I don't know what's been wrong with me the last few days. My mood has not been a pleasant one. It could have something to do with the fact that since the night I decided I was ready to have sex with Nix, he rejected me, and since then, I've been horny. Not horny as in read a hot book and have a horny ache. I mean all out, hot sex dreams and need-my-man's-cock-now horny. The past four days, the tension has been building and I'm ready to snap.

"Okay," he says carefully as he drops his towel and steps into his boxers. *Fuck me.* Even just watching him dress has me getting all kinds of angry horny. *Why can't we just have sex and release this frustration?* I still can't believe he rejected me. Short of begging, I don't know what he wants from me. Yeah, I might have flinched, but come on. Nerves about him seeing me again after everything we have been through were running rampant that night.

"Wanna tell me what's really goin' on here?"

"What?" I ask, not anticipating his question or the calmness in his voice. I quickly gather my thoughts. "Your pants and boots, I nearly fell over them. I've told you before to put your shit away." I throw his pants at him knowing an orgasm would fix my feral mood.

"You feel better?" he asks, placing his pants on the bed.

"No, actually, I don't," I snap, hating that even when I try to start on him, he still manages to stay calm.

"Well, have at it. Get it off your chest." He drops his ass to the bed and sits back waiting for it.

"Your fucking pants." I throw my arms out, pissed he's not listening to me.

"This is not about the fuckin' pants, Kadence. You've been givin' me attitude the past few days. You got somethin' on your mind?" He folds his arms across his bare, chiseled chest, pissing me off even more, because he's right. I do. But why does he have to fucking look so sexy when I'm giving him bitchy Kadence?

I stand there frozen, unsure how to bring up my needs—the

reason why I'm so bitchy is because I just need him.

"What is it, baby?" He stands and takes a step closer when I don't respond.

"Well," I begin, my breath coming out choppy as he comes to settle in front of me. I can see the droplets of water still pooled on his chest.

"Yes?" He smirks like he knows what his presence is doing to me.

"I really don't like it when you leave your clothes on the floor," I grind out, holding my own. *Jesus, what's wrong with me?* I have a moment to tell him what I need but I chicken out.

"What else do you need, Kadence?" He steps in closer, his body pressed against mine. The mix of his citrus shower gel stirs my nose.

"I—" I stop to breathe in the thick air. I can feel his arousal, and the tension between both of us is so palpable I have to take a second to breathe. "Nix—" I don't get another word out before his mouth is on mine. My hands move to his head, my fingers gliding through his dark hair. I'm lost in his lips as his hands move up my body. The heat of his warm skin against mine sends tingles down my spine, pushing me further and further into his body. I take a few steps back, the backs of my legs hitting the side of our bed. My fingers work their way down his shoulders, pulling him into me as I fall back. We land in the middle of the bed—him covering my body.

"This okay?" He pulls back, eyes searching. I nod, giving him the okay. Immediately, he rips my top up over my head. My nerves buzz in anticipation, but the need to connect with him overpowers it.

"Are you sure?" he asks again before touching me.

"Stop asking me," I snap, needing to feel, not think.

His movements stop and the air changes.

"Don't," I say, but my attitude ruins it. I know it. Covering myself up, I try to squash the feeling of disappointment down. I hate that this is what it has come to. *What have I done to us?*

"I'm sorry," I whisper, bringing my hand up to touch his face. His weight shifts, leaving me feeling cold.

"It's okay." He stands, looking unsure.

"Come back," I plead, needing his touch. I knew just by looking at him, my insecurities had passed onto him and I don't know how to fix it. What I do know, is that I don't just need my husband. I need the biker who pushed his way into my life. Somewhere along the way, I've lost him. I had pushed him away.

"I'm gonna go check on the kids." He steps back and my heart hurts.

"Don't leave. I'm sorry," I try again. "I need you, Nix."

"Not tonight, Kadence." He picks up his shirt and throws it in the basket, leaving me alone on the bed.

"Fuck!" I curse and sit up to replace my shirt. I should go after him, but knowing the type of man he is, it wouldn't be wise. I have to give him space and sort my own shit out. As much as my fears and insecurities are something I need to work through, I need him more. But to have him, I would have to let go and trust. Trust that Nix would have me.

I don't know why it's so hard.

7

Nix

"WHERE THE FUCK IS HE THEN?" I ASK THE TABLE OF MY brothers a few days later at one of our weekly club meets.

"He had a pick up, but Tiny says he's yet to show," Brooks explains.

Beau, like all the boys, is required to show up on time, but for some reason, we can't get a hold of him. Something's up. Beau has never missed a club meet.

"Well, someone better fuckin' find him." I try to let his fuck up slide. It's not like Beau fucks up regularly, but his not being here puts me on edge. If I was being honest, I know what's really putting me on edge. It's not because Beau is late. It's because of Kadence. I don't know what is happening between us, but it's fucking with my head. It's like every time I touch her and she flinches, I suffer a blow to my self-esteem.

"I'm worried about him," Sy speaks up. "He's getting attached."

"He's fuckin' Beau. He doesn't get attached," I counter.

"You didn't see him with Mackenzie. I've never seen him like that before."

"You think this new gig is getting to him?" The club has taken on a big role in helping Tiny get women out of abusive homes, especially Beau. I know that shit can be tough. I've been on a few runs, but Beau is fucking solid. *Isn't he?* I try to think of anything that I might have missed. Could his past be coming back to fuck with him?

"He's holding onto something that might be too close to home. I think the business with his sister fucked him up enough. He's reliving it over and over and he's gonna fucking snap. I can see it," Brooks says, giving his opinion.

"He's late for one meeting. He probably has a perfectly good reason. Let's not fuckin' lose our heads," I try to reason this time. Beau might be attached to this, but he would never jeopardize the club. He just wouldn't do it.

"Hunter, head out to the meet point. Keep Tiny updated." The rookie stands and nods, leaving without a word.

"Let's start. Got fucking shit to do. So how's Liquid? You get the staff all sorted?" I turn to Jesse. Dealing with his staffing issues is going to fucking kill me.

"Got a new girl." He nods.

"You gonna fuck this one?" Sy asks, trying to get a reaction.

"Fuck off." He smiles, but I ignore it. He's probably had her and her fucking best friend already. "Just because you three are fucking whipped." He nods to the remaining three of us left at the table.

50

"We're not fuckin' whipped," I snap. I don't hold back my attitude, or the fact he is pissing me off.

"Hey, I'm just saying. I'm not tied down. Don't have to deal with a tired wife, screaming kids. It must be hard. No wonder you're all cranky fuckers."

"Shut the fuck up, Jesse. You got no idea." I rub my face, his words hitting too close to home.

"I know the pussy I get never says no." He throws in and my fist clenches in my lap.

"Jesse, I suggest you shut the fuck up right fuckin' now," I warn, close to losing my shit.

"What's the matter, boss man? Your dick not getting wet?" My ass leaves the seat and my hands find his cut. I don't care if he's fucking with me, or just trying to get a reaction. I have him out of his chair and down on the table in less than five seconds.

"Whoa, whoa." Sy tries to pull me off, but I'm so close to punching this fucker; I won't be talked down.

"Too far?" he asks, a fucking grin on his face.

"Get the fuck out and go find Beau." I pull him up by his cut and push him toward the door.

"Got ya, but I just want to say, I didn't know Kadence was holding out on you." He smiles, fixing his messed-up shirt.

"Jesse, I swear to fuckin' Christ, get the fuck OUT!" My fist comes down in front of me. He shrugs, laughing as he leaves.

"Jesus, what the fuck was that?" Brooks asks, sitting back down.

"Nothin'," I reply, picking up the turned-over chair.

"You still haven't sorted business between you two?" Sy observes, hitting the nail on the head.

"Fuck." I shake my head. Not in the mood for this conversation.

"Jesus, I feel you brother." Sy sighs like he feels my pain.

"What? You haven't?" I count back the weeks since X was born.

"No, but it's been seven weeks this week. Gonna sort that shit out soon." He folds his arms across his chest like a smug bastard.

"Well, it's been eight fuckin' months."

"Fuck." Both men share my sentiments.

"No wonder your ass is fucking cranky." Brooks smirks.

"Not even a blow job?" Sy questions, still holding out hope for me.

"Fuckin' nothin'." I think back to the last time I tried to jack off. Got me no-fucking-where.

"Well, what the fuck is going on?" Brooks folds his arms, settling in for a good conversation. "Thought things were good?"

"Things are. She's doing a lot better. She's still on her meds, but it's like I got my Kadence back."

"Then what the fuck?" Sy looks as confused as Brooks.

"Don't know, but it's messin' with my head. She fuckin' tenses up and then I can't do it. Just can't fucking go through with it." I rest my elbows on the table, rubbing my hands over my face.

"What does she say?" Sy asks, looking concerned. I didn't think I'd be overly comfortable with talking about my shit, but if anyone can empathize with me, it's these guys. Brooks has been married the longest, and Sy brought Holly back when we thought we'd lost her forever. Surely, their experience amounts for something.

"Nothin'. We don't talk about it. She wants it and God knows I do, but she tenses when I touch her and I fuckin' lose it. Can't recover."

"You go hit the head to get your shit to wake up?" Brooks asks. As if I haven't tried that already.

"Believe me, I fucking tried. Can't even get it half-awake. It's a blow to my confidence, and then I'm like fuck it. I'm done."

"Shit." Sy whistles, learning the shit I'm dealing with.

"So fuckin' tell me how do I deal?" I ask, needing something.

"What are you afraid of?" Brooks asks this time.

"Not fuckin' afraid." The man in me stands up to his question, but something else tells me he's right. I am fucking scared.

They both look up; they know I'm full of it.

"Fine. I'm scared I'll fuck it up. She says she needs control, but I can't fucking hand that fucker over."

"Then don't!" Brooks practically shouts. "You fucking own that. Find a way to give it to her, in a way she thinks she's getting control."

Sy nods, agreeing with him.

"How the fuck do I do that?" I sit forward, interested in what he has to say. I can't help but think is this what chicks do with their fucking girly shit they talk about? I didn't know, but I was curious. I need to know how to fix mine and Kadence's problem, and I needed to fix it soon. I'm not gonna last much longer like this.

"I don't fucking know how. Let me know what you find out." He shrugs, shattering me without even knowing it.

"What about Viagra?" Sy asks.

"I'm not fuckin' takin' a blue pill, asshole."

"Why not? You have the problem with it staying up; there's your fix. Pop your pill and bend her over the kitchen counter. Problem solved." He nods, proud of himself, thinking he just fixed my issues.

"I'm not fuckin takin' it. I might have a problem gettin' there, but I'm not eighty fuckin' years old," I still argue as the seed of doubt is planted. I could take it and wouldn't have an issue with worrying about losing my hard on.

"He's fucking thinking of taking it." Sy smirks.

"You want some? I got it at home," Brooks offers, ignoring my scowl.

"Why the fuck do you have Viagra?" Sy asks.

"Thought I needed it few months back. Kelly was getting harder to keep up with."

"You use it?" I ask, interested in it more if he has tried it.

"Yeah, couple times. Good shit, but that was just a phase. Don't need it now."

I nod, taking in my options. I don't know what the fuck is wrong with me. I'm fucking forty this year. Is this what it has come to?

"You should do it," Sy encourages. "Take your old lady out, pop your pill, and claim your woman."

"Yeah, you got anything planned for Valentine's Day?" Brooks asks. *Fuck is that this week? Jesus.*

"I fuckin' do this, you don't breathe a word of it…" I can't believe what's coming out of my mouth.

"Scouts honor." Sy smirks.

"Yeah, last thing you need is Jesse giving you a hard time." Brooks laughs.

"I'm not fuckin' kiddin', assholes."

"Relax, fucker. I feel ya. Fuck, eight months, man. How are you still standing?" Brooks jokes but I ignore their laughs and pull out my phone to make a reservation for Valentine's Day. The boys don't leave; instead, they watch me sweet talk the waitress into giving me a table on their busiest night of the year.

"Who's gonna take the kids?" Sy asks after I start to feel good about my plan. *Shit.*

I pick up my phone and place a call to Red. He agrees to babysit which puts me back in a good mood. I grab my phone one more time and shoot Kadence a text.

Nix: You. Me. Valentine's Day. Be
ready at 7pm. You're mine.

"Right, this better fucking work." I look up at my brothers.

"It will, asshole." Sy stands from the club table. Our club meet is now a waste of time with no one around.

"Well, I hope for your sake it does." They both laugh, making their way back out to the bar.

"All right, back to business. You really worried about Beau?" I follow them out, done with talking about my less-than-stellar performance in the bedroom.

"You don't see him, Prez. Each time we go on a pickup, he gets worse. I'm just saying we need to watch him."

I nod, thinking back on the last few years. Since he lost his sister, he's been fucked up, but he's worked through a lot of his shit. We all have.

"Right, well, let's find him."

"Find who?" Beau walks in the door, right on cue and thirty minutes late.

"Where the fuck you been?" I turn to ask, but don't let him give me an answer before I'm barking at him again. "Who the fuck is that?" I point to the small woman by his side. Her face is down, hiding her eyes, but from the angle, I can still see how fucked-up she looks. Her blonde hair is matted, with blood stained through it, but what freaks me out the most is the baby she's holding in her arms.

"Fuck, Beau." I shake my head. I don't know who he brought into our club, but by the look on his face, we're in trouble. A whole lot of fucking trouble.

8

Kadence

"SO, WHAT DO YOU THINK HE HAS PLANNED?" HOLLY ASKS from my bed as I proceed to tear my closet apart. Both babies are sleeping: Low, in her crib, and X sleeping in the pack 'n play next to Holly. Z is over at a friend's house. Holly came over for lunch when I received the text from Nix telling me we have a date on Valentine's Day. At first, I was shocked. Nix hasn't spoken to me like that in months. His alpha-way of getting his point across has always been a weakness of mine, and reading it in his message, I could just hear his voice demanding that come Valentine's Day, I will be his. Insecurities or not, the way things have been between us these last few months had me jumping off the sofa and running straight to my closet at just the idea of a date

"Dinner? I don't know." I shrug, still not finding anything decent to wear. "I won't be going anywhere if I don't find anything."

"Oh, please. Have you seen your closet?"

"Oh, please. Have you seen my ass?" I counter, throwing a pair of jeans over my head.

"Jesus, did your ass ever fit into these?" Holly laughs when I growl. "Come on, Kadence, you look great."

"Doesn't change the fact nothing fits."

"You're being dramatic."

I roll my eyes as Holly holds my small jeans against her. "I say, forget stressing over the clothes. Let's talk about the lingerie."

"Oh, God. No. I'm not even looking in that drawer."

"Why not?"

"Holly, nothing I own will cover my boobs."

"Even better," she smiles, bouncing her brows.

"I wish I was like you." I drag my ass over to the bed and flop down.

"Kadence, I don't know what the issue is. You had a baby. It doesn't change anything. Nix still likes playing hide the salami." I give her a look telling her there has been no hiding of any one's salami.

"What is that look? You've had sex, right?" She drops the jeans, eyeing me closer. Well, there's no point lying.

"No."

"WHAT?" she shouts, stirring X for a moment.

"What?" I answer back.

"Kadence, what the hell is going on? How long has it been?"

"What, five months?" I shrug as if it's no big deal.

"Don't you dare lie to me." She crosses her arms, waiting for the truth.

"Ughhh," I groan, hating that I can't lie straight. "Fine. Eight months."

"Fuck, no wonder you're a—" I don't let her finish.

"A what?"

"Kadence, you have Nix, Nix *fucking* Knight in your bed every night, and you just shrug like it's no big deal?"

"Well, there's been a few things happening," I snap. A part of me agrees with her, but I can't help feeling defensive.

"Sorry, I didn't mean it like that." She moves toward me, awkwardness growing in the air. "You're feeling good now, right?"

"Yeah, we're in a good place. Low is good. She's doing really well. It's been so long. I just don't know what's happening. Every time we try, I tense. Nix freaks out and then the moment's over."

"Oh, God, girl. You need help."

"I know."

"So what's the issue?"

"I don't know. I freak out about my body. Maybe he won't find me attractive. I know he loves me, Holly, but I can't control what I feel inside. I've tried."

"Kadence, you're so messed up."

I look up at her, shocked she would throw that back at me.

"Oh, God, not like that," she rushes out, and I smile carefully. Only she would put her foot in her mouth.

"I know it's messed up. I just don't know how to fix it. I can't relax enough. It's just too much pressure."

"I understand pressure, Kadence. When Sy and I first had sex after losing the baby, it was after a long build-up of sexual tension. I get your insecurities. I do. But Nix is your husband. Trust me. He's not looking at you thinking your thighs are thicker. He doesn't count your stretchmarks, nor is he worried that your boobs are bigger.

Okay, he is totally loving your boobs, but that's not the point. He's looking at his wife, the mother of his child. He loves you, Kadence."

"It's more than all those things, Holly. I feel like it's bigger than that. What if we can't come back? What if we're not those people anymore?"

"Why are you talking like you're not the same person, Kadence?" she snaps. Her frustration isn't lost on me; I've seen the same look on Nix's face.

"Because I'm not, Holly. I'll never be that person again."

"Are you sure? 'Cause the Kadence I know is still sitting in front of me. She might be scared, hell, even a little uptight, but she's there. Don't try to deny it. I've watched Nix bring you to your highest, hold you in your darkest, save you from your lowest and he has never faltered. He has never looked away, or said it was too hard. Your man worships you. How can you not see this? Open your eyes, woman. You are *here*. You are here and you are living it."

She's right. I do know this. Jesus, I live this. Maybe I just needed to hear it from a different perspective. Yeah, my body has changed, but it wasn't perfect to begin with. The way Nix looks at me should be enough to prove how much he wants me, but I guess the last few months I lost a lot more than I thought I did.

"You're right. I know that man loves me, Holly, but I'm afraid I've pushed him too hard, for too long." I wipe at my face in anger, my tears failing to wash me clean of any wrongdoing. We've come so far. I know that connection we've always had isn't lost. It's just sitting hidden; hidden under my insecurities, under my own doubt. I'm the one holding back. How could I ever doubt Nix?

"Well, lucky for you, you're married to Nix Knight, and you could probably push him off a cliff and he'll come right back."

I smile at her analogy because I know she's right. Nix has proven himself over and over.

"Now, come on. We need a full makeover and we need to clean the cobwebs."

"What cobwebs?" I ask, taking a steady breath. I'm ready to do whatever I need to do in order to reclaim my man.

"From your vagina, Kadence."

I laugh at her forwardness but don't argue, because I agree. I need this. I need to let go, to help us get back to where we were.

"Okay, let's do this." I nod, ready for Holly's expertise.

"Good. Now show me this lingerie." She moves back to the bed with her own smile on her face. "I want to see boob. Lots of boob." Her laugh almost wakes X, and still I don't argue. I follow her orders, praying her confidence pays off.

Dear God, it better. I have a date with my husband.

With Nix Knight, President of the Knights Rebels.

God, I've missed that man. I think I should stop trying to push him off the cliff.

★★★

"Hey, baby," Nix whispers as he climbs in bed behind me. "Did you get my text?"

"Yeah," I yawn, turning to face him. "What time is it?"

"Just after two."

"Everything okay?"

"Fuckin' shit goin' down. Club business."

"Anything I need to know?" I ask, knowing he hates talking shop, but he will share if he thinks I need to know.

"Beau brought a woman and kid to the clubhouse yesterday." He rests his head back against the headboard.

"One of his pickups?"

"Yeah, only this one belongs to another club."

"What other club?"

"The Warriors."

"Shit." The Warriors are a rival club, one the Knights have always had trouble with. They struck a truce last year and now this shit? This isn't good at all.

"Yeah," he sighs. "Gotta shit storm brewing. I can feel it."

"What was he thinking?"

"He wasn't. Says he had the opportunity to save her, so he took it."

"So, what now?" Panic rises in my chest. King and his men might have come to a truce with Nix and the Rebels, but you mess with them, a truce means nothing.

"We wait. Nothing connects us to her. Got her set up at the safe house," He assures me, pulling me into his body. "I do need you to get some baby shit together though."

"Okay. I'll ask Holly, too." I rest my head against his chest.

"Good, Jesse is gonna head up tomorrow."

"Is this bad, Nix? Should I be worried?" I close my eyes, waiting to hear his response.

"You have nothing to worry about. King and I are good. As long as we keep her hidden, it's not gonna come back to us."

"I don't like this, Nix."

"I know, but trust I got this. Not gonna let anythin' happen to you, okay?"

Trust. That trust word again. The first step at getting back to where we were.

"I trust you, Nix."

"Good. Now go back to sleep. We have a hot date tomorrow." I smile into his chest. Yes, a hot date. How could I forget?

"I'm very excited," I yawn, shifting back into a good position.

"You should be," he jokes, and I chuckle. "Don't worry, babe. I got you." He pulls me closer to his front.

"You always have me," I whisper, feeling myself fall into the dark bliss.

"Never not gonna have you, Kadence. Would fuckin' die before I didn't have you. Now go back to sleep," he orders again, and that small flutter of lust stirs in me.

Yes, that trust, it's coming back.

9

Nix

"OH, FOR FUCK'S SAKE." I SLAM THE PHONE DOWN THE next afternoon and walk into the hall, kicking the first thing I see—a fuckin' stool.

"What's up your ass now?" Jesse asks from the sofa, sitting up from the racket. He just got back to the clubhouse from his trip to Beau, dropping the baby supplies off to the safe house.

"Fuckin' Red is sick. Just cancelled on me."

"Cancelled what?" Jesse asks.

"Shit. What about Kadence's parents?" Brooks joins the conversation, walking out from behind the bar.

"They're away for the weekend," I answer, ignoring Jesse.

Fuck.

My fist slams down on the bar in frustration.

"What's got your panties in a twist?" Jesse moves off the sofa and comes to stand by me.

"There's always—" Brooks' nods to Jesse.

"Fuck, no." I watch as Jesse tries to figure out what we're talking about.

"He's your only hope," Brooks pushes.

"Someone fucking tell me what is happening," Jesse interrupts again, this time getting Brooks' attention.

"Nix needs a sitter. You're it." Brooks slaps Jesse on the back and walks back to the bar.

"So, you finally need me," he says, no doubt ready to rub it in.

"No," I repeat, not in the mood for Jesse's shit.

"Why not?" He folds his arms across his chest and cocks a brow.

"Yeah, why not? You're desperate. Everyone's out or busy," Brooks repeats Jesse's question, his grin pissing me off. Fuck, he's right, and the last thing I want to do is cancel on Kadence.

"Fuck, fine. Can you watch the kids, Jesse?" I ask, watching his shit-eating grin spread wide.

"Ask nicer."

"Fuck you, Jesse."

He doesn't respond, just waits quietly while I rack my brain thinking who else can watch them, but I've got nothing. *Fuck.*

"Fine. Jesse, can you please watch Low and Z?" I practically have to bite the inside of my cheek when asking.

"I have a date, but—" he shrugs, but I stop him from going on.

"No."

"You didn't let me finish."

"You're not fucking some whore on my sofa as my kids sleep

upstairs." He watches me carefully. I know he's fucking with me, but this week has been fucking hell and I need this night with Kadence.

"Fine. I'll do it for twenty an hour."

"Fuck off." I hit him over the head before walking away. "Be at my house at six. Don't be fuckin' late," I warn, heading back into my office. Sometimes I really fucking wonder about the asshole.

"You owe me," he calls out after me.

"Call it even after the shit you bring me daily." He doesn't respond. He gets it.

"Nix, I left the important info on your desk," Brooks adds before I turn the corner.

"Info?" I look back, confused as hell. He raises his brows, waiting for me to get it. *Oh, shit.*

"Yep, thanks. Got it." I nod, walking back into my office.

"I want dinner too," Jesse calls out one more demand, but instead of replying, I slam my door. It's probably the worst idea to ask Jesse to watch the kids. Kadence might flip, or she might not. I'll probably kill him before he even gets to the house anyway.

★★★

"Ten minutes, Kadence, or we're gonna be late," I yell from the bottom of the stairs later that night.

"I don't know much about dating, since I'm only eleven, but I don't think you should do that," Z says to the TV screen as he plays one of his Xbox games with Jesse.

"Yeah, I'm with you there, bud." Jesse fist bumps Z while Low sits beside them in her walker.

I ignore my son's advice 'cause he's probably right, and decide to give Jesse one more warning. "You better not fuck this up, Jesse."

"Nix, language," Kadence reprimands me.

I turn and watch her take the last few steps down the stairs. "Jesus." I clear my throat and turn, taking a good look. She's wearing a pair of black jeans, practically painted on, and an off-the-shoulder top that hugs her tits and shows off her collarbones. Her hair is down in soft curls, just the way I fucking love it.

"Jesus, Joseph, and doggy-style Mary." Jesse whistles from the sofa.

"Jesse!" Kadence scolds, breaking me from my stare.

"What? I was just giving Nix some words. He looks lost."

"The kids." Her eyes bug out, worried Z might have been listening but he's too focused on the game to pay attention, missing out on the adult conversation.

"I got them, Kadence, all good." Jesse smiles his stupid smile and goes back to the game. She looks back to me, but I'm still stuck in the moment, relishing what a fucking knockout my wife is.

"You okay?" she asks, picking up her purse.

"Yeah. Just not sure if I'm going to be able to handle you on the back of my bike."

"We're taking the bike?" Her voice sounds excited, shocked even.

"Yeah, that okay?"

"It's great." She smiles and my gut twists. *Jesus.*

"You remember what I told you, Jesse?" She walks toward Low to say goodbye.

"Yep, got it. You do know I'm a decorated ex-marine, firefighter and badass biker. I got this, sweetheart."

"I know, I know." She bends down and kisses Low. I was surprised by her reaction when I told her Red pulled out and Jesse was in. She didn't seem too worried. I think she likes Jesse more than me some days.

"Okay, let's go." She moves to Z, kissing him briefly before coming back to me.

"Call us if you need anything." I nod to Jesse.

"I got it. Go."

"Yeah, Dad, go," Z repeats.

We walk out to my bike in silence. The only sound in the air is Kadence's fuck-me heels clicking on the pavement.

"You okay?" I ask when I place the helmet on her head.

"Yeah." She nods but I can see a small amount of unease in her.

"You look fuckin' beautiful." I kiss her hard and her hands come around my waist, pulling me closer.

"You look sexy." She bites at my lip, sending pain from my mouth straight to my dick.

Fuck, I forgot about the fucking pill. "You ready?" I cut the kiss short, pulling back to help her on my bike.

"Where we going?"

"Got us a table at Moda."

"You got a table at Moda?" Shock laces her voice as a smile graces her face. I can't blame her for being shocked. A man like me, eating at fucking Moda. I wouldn't normally, but my woman deserves a special night out, so I'll eat at the stupid over-priced place.

"Yeah, baby." I place a kiss on her lips and tap her helmet. She doesn't reply. The huge grin is enough to tell me I did good.

"Do you think the kids will be okay?" She looks back at the house. I don't have to see her face to know she's freaking a little.

"Yeah, baby. You know I give Jesse shit, but I trust him with my life."

"Yeah, me too." She turns back and gives me one of her smiles.

"Let's go." I straddle the bike in front of her, reaching my arm back to move her closer.

"Is it weird that I'm nervous?" she whispers close to my ear. I turn my body to face her. Her worries are my worries. Her nerves are mine.

"Baby, you haven't been on the back of my bike in over a year. I'd say it's normal." I try to reassure her, but my words do the opposite.

"Has it been that long?"

"Yeah," I nod, hating the truth of that one word.

"Damn." She looks down at her hands. I twist further around, forcing her chin up with my finger.

"There's been a lot of things we haven't done this year, baby, and that's okay. We don't have to rush. We've got forever." I lean in and kiss her.

"I just wish our journey was different." She doesn't look me in the eyes, and it guts me that she thinks that.

"It might have been a tough year, Kadence, but it's been the best one of my life. You gave me Low, gave Z a mom, and made us a family again. We might have lost ourselves along the way, but we're findin' those people again, and I don't think anythin' could take that away."

Her eyes shine with unshed tears so I kiss her again, stopping with the mushy shit.

"Let's go." I smile, turn back and start the bike. The engine roars to life as Kadence's fingers dig into my cut and I'm thrown back to the first night I had her on the back of my bike. The Kadence from that night, only slightly resembles the woman now sitting behind me, but I don't let it get to me. Instead, I focus on giving my wife one hell of a date. Later, I will worry about bringing the sassy, fiery woman back to me.

★★★

"What do you mean you don't have me down?" My voice rises

and Kadence's grip in my hand gets tighter.

"I'm sorry, but I don't have your reservation here, sir." The young blonde standing in front of me tells me for the second time.

"Well, I called and booked it. So I suggest you find a table for my wife and me. *Now*," I grind out as she nods carefully.

"Give me a moment, sir." She turns and leaves us standing there.

We walked in two minutes ago, after a quick detour to the clubhouse to pick up the pill Brooks left me. I didn't tell Kadence what I was doing. She waited outside while I raced in to get it. I didn't ask Brooks when to take it, so instead of calling him, I quickly googled it on my phone. Some people said to take it a few hours before you planned on needing it, so I quickly slipped it down without any water and met Kadence at the front.

"It's okay, Nix. We don't have to eat here." She pulls on my arm, but I don't give a shit what the waitress is saying. I booked it.

"Yes, we do. I fuckin' booked it." I keep my eye on the girl as she moves through the restaurant back to us.

"I'm sorry, sir, but we can't help you."

My fist comes down on the front desk causing her to step back.

"Damn it," I curse, watching a man walk forward.

"I'm going to have to ask you to leave."

"This is bullshit," I begin, but Kadence steps in between me and the fucking punk.

"Let's go, baby."

"Kadence."

"No, let's go to the bar. It will be like our first date."

"You kicked me in the balls our first date, baby," I remind her, still eyeing off the fucker who thinks he's tough.

"Well, if you don't move your ass from here, I'll kick you again."

I smirk at her sass. "You sure?" I look down at her to get a read on what she's thinking.

"Please, it will be fun," she responds, so I don't argue. I take her hand and walk out. The club bar is only a block down on Main, so we decide to walk.

"You always act like this on a date?" she jokes, nestling closer to me under the warmth of my arm.

"Only with girls I like." I try to be smooth and it gets me an eye roll. My favorite kind.

"You really want to eat here?" I ask again, when we get to the front door.

"Yesss." She drags it out and pulls me inside.

The bar is busy. The table we sit at every time we come in is occupied, but as soon as Hunter sees us, he clears them out.

"Hunter doesn't have a date tonight?" Kadence asks, sliding into the booth.

"Don't give a fuck if Hunter has a date." I slide in after her. She shakes her head but doesn't reply.

"So not what I was expecting when I wanted to take you out." I lean down and run my nose along her hairline.

"I think this place is fine, Nix."

I nod to Hunter as he brings us both our usual drinks and a menu.

"You hungry?" she asks, looking over the menu. I don't know why she bothers. She orders the same thing every time we come.

"Starved." My hand moves down to her thigh and my cock stirs in my jeans. This is what I miss, just being with each other. Comfortable and in the moment.

"You keep groping me and you'll end up like the first time we met here," she sasses, and I can't help but grin.

"You mean in my bed, with your pussy milking my cock?" The hiss of her breath stirs my dick, and I hold in the groan at seeing her nostrils flare. Fuck, this woman has no idea what she does to me.

"No, I meant the scene where you got kneed in the balls." She smirks when the waitress comes to take our order. I remember that night clearly. The night I fell in love with my wife. I don't know if it was the knee to my balls, or the way I watched her eyes light up after going on her first ride on the back of my bike. I knew that night, when I held her in my arms, I was going to love her. I knew then it wouldn't be easy. With a woman like Kadence, you wouldn't want love to be easy. I knew going in it would be fierce, raw, and by fucking God, this woman has given me everything and then more.

"I fuckin' love you. Do you know that?" I stop our playful banter and turn serious on her. "You still ruin me, woman, fuckin' sittin' here with your sexy self. I still can't believe you're mine, you know that? You're fuckin' *mine*."

"Stop it." She smiles but it's an awkward one, as if the compliment makes her uncomfortable.

"I know we have a long way to go, baby, fuck I do. But I'm tellin' you now, your man tells you you're sexy, you don't fuckin' smile like you don't believe it. You hear me?" The air between us changes, like a switch has been flipped, and her eyes come back to life. And fuck me if it ain't the most amazing fucking thing I've ever seen. "You do that shit again, I'll fuckin' bend you over the nearest surface and spank your hot little ass. You hear me?" I watch as her lips quiver at my tone. "Kadence," I push when she doesn't answer.

"You wouldn't dare." She swallows and I know I have her attention. I twist my body to face her and lean into her space. "Try me." I don't know what the fuck I'm doing, or if I'm doing it right, but something in the air tonight tells me this is what she needs. Maybe I'm going about it the wrong way, but I'm at a point where I don't care. This is not just what Kadence needs, but what I need.

"Let's dance." She breaks the moment and moves into me. I know she's trying to escape our table, but I don't argue or push with my previous threats, just pull her out and follow her to the dance floor. The music is slow, and normally I wouldn't dance to this shit, but tonight is about Kadence and with the fuck-up at Moda, I'm not about to deny her.

She turns to face me and slowly begins to move.

"Don't go all shy on me." I pull her into me.

"I didn't think this through," she complains, but I won't let her backtrack.

"Just follow my lead," I tell her and move to face her away with her back to my front. After two songs, I'm regretting my decision as Kadence's ass moves faster against me.

"Fuck, baby. Let's go back." I groan as my cock throbs even harder. Fuck, I haven't felt this hard in such a long time.

"What's wrong?" She turns and looks down at me straining in my jeans.

"All good, baby." I adjust myself, feeling it grow even more. Jesus, that pill is fucking dangerous.

"You sure you're okay?" Kadence asks. Her amusement turns into concern when we walk back to the table. I squeeze my eyes shut as my head becomes lost in the fog of my arousal.

"I really need to fuck you," I admit.

"I'm sure you can wait." She smirks, patting my leg. My hand covers hers, stopping her from pushing me over the edge.

"I don't think you get me. If I don't fuck you soon, this is going to be bad." I realize no truer words have been spoken as I say them. My heart rate picks up and my whole body tingles. Jesus, I shouldn't have taken that Viagra.

Taking her hand in mine, I pull her out of the booth and drag her out the door—leaving our food and drinks behind.

"Nix, what's going on? We didn't even get to eat."

"I took something and if I don't fuck you soon, I'm gonna fucking explode," I explain, pulling her along at a faster pace. I doubt she gets the severity in my voice, but her rubbing her ass against me was a bad idea.

"What did you take?" She stops in front of my bike, pulling her arm from my grasp.

"Just something to bring my boy to attention."

"You took Viagra!" Her voice rings out on the sidewalk.

"Shit, tell the fuckin' town." I place the helmet on her head. "Yes, took something. It's no big deal. I just need to fuck you now, so get that sweet ass on the bike. I'm taking you home."

She moves to argue, but I stop her. "Swear to Christ, woman. Get your ass on the fuckin' bike now or I'm takin' you right here." She stands there shocked, taking in the seriousness of my voice, before looking down at my bike. I don't know what she's thinking, don't know if I'm pushing her too far, but I wasn't lying when I told her I'd fuck her against my bike. If she even hesitates, it's a done fuckin' deal.

10

Kadence

I SWALLOW PAST THE LUMP IN MY THROAT AT HIS CONFESSION, and squeeze my legs together at his threat.

"Kadence," he pushes, clearly in pain.

"Okay, okay."

He takes my hand and helps me onto the bike. I have to bite my lip to hold in the laugh. This date is interesting to say the least.

"If you had a skirt on tonight, I don't even think I'd make it home," he says, climbing on and revving the throttle; the loud rumble of the pipes filling my ears and taking me to a place that only Nix and his bike can take me.

I move forward and wrap my arms around him. "Lucky I didn't.

Last thing we need tonight is an arrest," I joke as we take off. I don't hear his reply, but going by the tightness in his jeans, I know this ride will be an uncomfortable one. Trying not to worry about what is coming, I close my eyes and rest my head on his back.

After a five-minute drive, we pull up at the front of the clubhouse.

"What are we doing here?" I ask when he shuts his bike off, and helps me down.

"Not even gonna make it home." He pulls me along and I struggle to keep up, tripping on my own feet.

"Come on, Nix. It can't be that bad," I laugh, not believing the situation.

The clubhouse is quieter than normal, but a few people are still hanging around.

"Everyone, out now!" Nix booms, standing in the middle of the main room. I know it's a ridiculous demand, but the men move fast, with no complaints, and I stand here getting more turned on. Oh, Jesus, what are they thinking? After a few goodbyes, and knowing looks, we're left alone.

I walk up to the bar and pour myself a whiskey while Nix locks the doors.

"Thank fuck they're gone." He comes back and I turn.

"It was a bit extreme, no?" I look around the now empty clubhouse. He doesn't answer, just watches me carefully.

"I'm gonna fuck you now, Kadence." He finally speaks, the thick air around us, growing as each second ticks by. "Your choice where. In my bed, over the bar, or on the pool table." His voice is gravelly, and I don't know if he's just too turned on to talk, or if it's the drugs he took.

"You sure you're okay, Nix?" I ask, half turned-on, half really worried.

"Yeah, baby. I'm fine." He clears his throat and shakes his head.

"Nix, I'm worried," I begin, but he doesn't listen. His jeans drop to the floor, his shirt is ripped off next, and in no less than thirty seconds, he stands before me naked with the angriest erection I've ever seen.

"Jesus, Nix." I can't hold in the gasp, my breath leaving me in one, fast whoosh.

"Fuck, I know, baby, and you're gonna take it," he warns, gripping himself in his hand. "No bullshit tensing and no pulling away. I'm gonna take you the way you need to be taken, Kadence, and you're gonna beg me for more. You understand me?" And just like that, he sends another thrill straight to my pussy. I've missed this Nix. Bossy, sexy, Nix.

I nod, knowing words would be pointless.

"You didn't answer my first question, so I'll choose." He steps closer. "Strip and bend over the pool table," he demands, still stroking his cock. A small part of me wants to argue, the look of unease over his face is enough to worry, but my need to have him out-weighs any concern.

Bending over, I remove my heels and slowly peel my jeans down my legs. I push all insecurities out of my head and come back to full height. *You can do this, Kadence.*

"Put your heels back on." This time his voice scratches.

"Do you need some water, Nix?" He shakes his head and points to the table. Instead of arguing, I do as he asks, stepping back into my heels.

"Shirt too." He moves closer and my body trembles at his command. I take a breath and keep my eyes on the floor, pulling my top up over my head.

"Look at me," he demands, pushing me deeper into his arousal.

"Fuckin' sexy bra, but you need to lose it." His eyes move over the lingerie set Holly and I spent half a day trying to find. I continue to follow his instructions, dropping my bra to the rest of the pile.

"Now, drop your panties, walk your fine ass over to the pool table, and show me your pussy." I don't let myself get caught up in nerves. On shaky legs, I do as I'm told. I let Holly's words hold me together, while Nix's demands try to break me down.

"Baby," Nix groans when I plant my hand on the green felt, and spread my legs. I feel him move in behind me, his front grazing my back.

"Fuckin' missed this, baby. You perched over like this, showin' me your pussy. All fuckin' pink and pretty." The feather touch of his finger runs through my wetness and the simple touch nearly brings me undone.

"I'm gonna eat you, Kadence. Gonna fuckin' eat you like a starved man," he promises. His voice rises up to me from the low position he moves to. Then his mouth is on me. Warm. Wet. Brutal.

I buck as his tongue flicks my clit. The feel of his chin all rough and prickly, dangles me over the edge of pleasure and pain.

"Nix." The moan leaves my mouth without me realizing it. I'm consumed by this man. Even thinking is too much when his mouth is on me.

"God, baby, I miss that sound," he confesses against me. The grumble of his voice vibrating my core.

"Yes, Nix. There, oh, God. Yes." My orgasm runs through me. Hard. Fast. Raw.

Excitement fills every inch of my needy body as the pleasure pushes me over. Every nerve in me comes to life, igniting me, reclaiming me.

"That's it, baby," Nix whispers in my ear. His fingers replace his mouth as one hand moves up and pinches my nipple.

"Gonna fuck you now, baby, and you're gonna take it like a good girl. You got me?"

"Yeah." I moan my answer when his hardness moves through my folds, then sinks home in one hard thrust.

"Jesus." We both groan as his cock throbs and my walls pulse to accommodate him.

"Fuck, Kadence," he growls. I squeeze him in my grip as he slides out then pushes back in. The sting of him stretching me is long forgotten when his movements milk the pleasure from me.

"Harder," I cry as my body builds, greedy for my moment of ecstasy. I've waited too long for this high, nothing will stop me from racing toward it again.

"Harder?" His question is forced out over the sound of his balls slapping against me.

"Fuck me harder, Nix," I beg, scratching at the felt under my fingers. Each thrust pushes my hips into the side of the pool table. I know tomorrow I'll be bruised, but I've missed this. Missed Nix and missed our connection so much, I don't even care. I can't care because I have my man inside of me. Fucking me like I've never been fucked before. That's all that matters.

"Fuck, baby. Hold on," Nix's strained voice warns, and his speed spirals out of control. Each deep thrust pushes me head first into a heart shattering, soul changing and mind blowing bliss.

I let the room around us fade. I let all my insecurities go. I let the past wash over me, the ugliness I've lived fade, and in return, the goodness we once had shines bright. Fuck, I've missed my man.

"Jesus, Kadence." Nix's orgasm ends in an almighty roar. "Welcome back, baby," he pants as he pulls my head back and takes my mouth in his Nix-way of dominating me.

"You can say that again," I pant against his lips. My breathing comes back to normal, but I know my body won't recover so quickly.

We stay connected and in the moment until I feel like I can no longer stand. "Nix, let me up," I complain, my legs shaking under my own weight.

"Hmmm," he replies still planted deep.

"Nix." I twist up to see what he's doing, but don't get far when he falls to the floor. "Nix." I half laugh, half choke at his fall.

"Fuck," he groans and I fall down next to him.

"Are you okay?" I move to lay over his chest.

"I don't know. My dick feels numb." I lift my head and look down at his still hard, angry looking cock.

"Fuck, Nix, it's so big."

"What the fuck does that mean?"

I look down at it again. "I mean," I giggle when he smacks my ass, "it just doesn't normally look so big."

"Oh, it's big, woman. Tell me how much you love it." He rolls over me, covering me with his weight.

"Okay, it's big, but that," I look down as it stands to attention against my stomach, "is a monster."

"I love it when you talk about my cock with so much love." His teeth sink into the side of my neck.

"I think I love your angry cock," I counter as his mouth moves down my neck, along my collarbone.

"I think my angry cock wants you."

"Again?"

He doesn't answer; instead, he brings his fingers between my legs, and slides back inside me. I try not to laugh at the predicament we find ourselves in. We go from not having sex in months to twice in the matter of ten minutes.

"Sweetheart, you have no idea." He looks at me with such love I don't know how I ever doubted him. Doubted us.

"Show me what you've got, Mr. Knight."

"With pleasure, Mrs. Knight."

★★★

"What do you mean it won't go down?" Brooks asks down the cell phone hours later as we sit in the hospital cubicle waiting for a doctor. I look down at Nix's lap and see his cock still standing to attention.

"I mean, it won't go down," I try to explain over the sound of Nix groaning in pain.

"Fuck."

"Yeah, fuck," I snap back. "I can't believe you gave it to him, Brooks." On the way to the hospital, Nix told me about Brooks hooking him up.

"Can we not have this conversation," Nix moans next to me.

"I don't know how long we're going to be, so can you check on Jesse for us?"

"Yeah, I'll call him," Brooks agrees, and I feel a little bad that his night with Kelly is messed up, but at least he's not in Nix's position.

"Thanks, I'll keep you posted." I hang up and sit back down to wait for the doctor.

"I can't believe you took it. What were you thinking, Nix?"

"I don't know why you're pissed. It's my cock," Nix moans. The longer his hard-on stays, the more in pain he seems to be.

"You're right. It's your dick that's gonna have to get a fucking needle in it," I snap. I'm not sure what I'm really angry at; the fact Nix thought he needed a pill to get hard to have sex with me, or that our date is over. I think more that our amazing date is over.

After taking me over the pool table and again on the floor, we spent the evening talking, eating and playing pool. It was as if time had never moved between us. We talked about the past, the kids, how far we had come. We made promises that we would make more time for ourselves. We shared our fears and talked of what our future holds. We laughed. I cried. We made love and vowed to always come back to each other. We connected on a level we never had before and I finally felt like we had found each other again. Then after all of that, when the sun was threatening to rise, when our children would soon be waking, Nix took me again. Only instead of ending our perfect night making love, something went terribly wrong. Now, sitting in ER with a raging hard-on that won't go away, my husband waits for news I don't think he's prepared for.

"You don't have to remind me." He holds out his hand, waiting for me to take it.

"Oh, I don't think you have to worry about that, Nix. I'm sure the boys will have that sorted." I snort, knowing if word gets around to Jesse, Nix will never live this shit down.

"Kadence, I was only trying to make it good for you, baby," he explains and I don't have anything to say to that. It's always been good. He definitely doesn't need it, but I know that my insecurities, helped fuel his, so I can't blame him.

"Mr. Knight?" An older male doctor walks in before I can respond.

"Yep, that's me." Nix nods, trying not to let the pain show over his face.

"Why, Mr. Knight, are you happy to see me?" The doctor looks down at my husband's cock. I try not to let it affect me; try to look away, but one look at Nix's face and the laughter comes. I'm a bad person, laughing at the inappropriate joke the old doctor cracks, but I can't help it.

"Shut your mouth, woman," Nix warns, not one bit impressed. I cover my mouth to mask the snort and watch him turn back to face the older man.

"So, what seems to be the problem?" the doctor asks, looking down at his chart.

"I think my wife broke my cock, Doc." The room fills with laughter while Nix groans in pain.

"For that comment, I will tell Jesse," I tease, not really meaning it.

"Do it and I will spank you," he growls through his pain and just like that, Nix and Kadence are back. We might have had a long way to go, sitting in an ER room with a broken dick, but that didn't matter. None of it mattered, because Nix had me, and I had Nix. We had come full circle. We struggled and we fell, but we did it with an unconditional love. We came back to each other when it was all said and done.

Our love wasn't a fight, but something worth fighting for.

We would always be something worth fighting for.

Epilogue

Kadence
six months later

"DO YOU REMEMBER THAT TIME NIX BROKE HIS DICK?" Jesse asks, causing everyone to start laughing.

"Shut the fuck up, Jesse." Nix growls beside me while I try to hold in my laugh.

"What? It was ages ago." He ignores his prez's death stare and continues to tell his new woman the story of how Nix ended up in the hospital after taking Viagra.

"You should have seen it, babe. So fucking bad. Had to get that shit drained."

Bell, Jesse's new woman, laughs next to him causing Nix to stand up.

"It was Kadence's fault." He points down to me, and a grin spreads across his face. "She broke it, not me."

"I did not!" I half shout and half laugh at the ridiculous conversation we are having.

We've just finished dinner, one of our monthly family dinners where all the guys from the clubhouse come over and devour my lasagna. Everyone came over tonight: Sy, Holly and baby X, Kelly and Brooks, Jesse and his woman Bell—even Beau turned up with a smile.

"Admit it. Your pussy broke my dick." He folds his arms across his chest and the guys all snort.

"Well, if you didn't have problems getting it up…" I leave the statement hanging as the air goes dangerously quiet.

"Did she just say that?" Brooks asks the table, but I can't answer cause Nix slowly turns to face me. My eyes lock onto his narrowed ones and I know I shouldn't have gone there.

"You will pay for that." He steps forward and I push back my chair trying to escape. "Everyone out. *Now*. I need to teach my wife a lesson." He snags me around the waist, heaves me out of the chair and throws me over his shoulder.

"Put me down, you big old lug." I smack his tight ass, and try to wiggle out of his grasp.

"Shhh, baby. You'll wake the kids."

"You're just going to leave us here?" Jesse calls out as Nix carries me through the glass doors back into the house.

"Yep, lock up." Nix continues to walk, ignoring our guests, and heading up the stairs.

"Nix," I complain but it only gets me a smack on my ass.

"You wanna see how hard I can get it up, baby?" he rumbles and I know I'm in trouble. Teasing Nix about that night six months ago never gets me anywhere. Even though I promised never to tell Jesse about the events of that Valentine's Day date, Brooks didn't make such promises, and since then, Nix hasn't lived it down.

"You know I was playing, baby." I laugh as he kicks our bedroom door open.

"Oh, I know. Now it's my turn to play." He throws me down on the bed and steps back.

"What are you going to do to me?" I come up on my elbows and watch him lose his cut and shirt.

"No questions." His tone tells me he's not kidding, and his stare makes me ache. Bossy Nix is coming out to play tonight.

"Shouldn't we wait until everyone has left?" I can't help myself. I ask a question when I shouldn't. The sounds of everyone packing up downstairs won't drown out what we are about to do.

"They're leavin'. Stand up and strip." He drops his boxers and I don't disobey. Doing what he asks, I unzip my dress and let it fall to my feet, exposing my fully naked body.

"Jesus, fuck. You've been naked under that fucking dress all night?" His erection grows as he stands there watching me.

I nod, giving him a sly grin.

We've come a long way in the last six months. We had a rough year, but looking back, we wouldn't be where we are if we didn't experience it.

"Do you know how much I love your body?" He steps closer, our bodies almost touching.

"No. Tell me how much."

"So fucking beautiful," he murmurs, his eyes roaming my now larger, plumper breasts. "Fuck, baby." His cursing comes out as half growl, half moan. "What I wouldn't do to sink my cock between these." He dips his head, pulling one nipple into his mouth. His hand moves to the opposite breast, massaging and tweaking as he sucks. Jesus, the pleasure of his warm mouth and the pain of my sensitive nipples is too much. A slow moan builds in the back of my throat; the image of him releasing himself over me plays out in my head. "You gonna let me fuck your tits, baby?" His hand finds his cock. I keep my eyes trained on his grip, each full and deliberate stroke pushing me deeper into his spell.

Fuck.

"Why the sudden interest in my boobs, Nix?" I lock my brow and watch him lick his lips.

"Been dreamin' about sliding my cock between these babies for months. Think I'm takin' that chance before you lose them."

"I don't think they are going away." I laugh and he lifts my chin.

"Fuck, I wish that was true, but they're already gettin' smaller."

"You think?" I ask, excited that the exercise and healthy eating I've been doing is finally starting to work.

"Don't sound so excited about it." He pushes me back on the bed and follows me down.

"I am. I've been working hard." He knows how hard I work. Not only for fitness, but for a healthy mind.

"You know you don't need that shit. You're fuckin' sexy."

"Of course you say that. But you have to. You're my husband."

"I don't have to fuckin' say anythin'. I'm sayin' it 'cause it's the truth."

"Well, lucky I'm not doing it for you." I reach up and bring my lips to his.

"Whatever makes you happy, baby."

"You make me happy, Nix."

"Do I?" He looks down at me seriously for a second. "'Cause for a long time there, I didn't know if I did, and nothin' has ever cut so deep knowin' I couldn't bring you happiness." I move up to my elbow, needing to be in his space.

"You have always brought me happiness, Nix. Always." I kiss him. Needing to show how much I mean it.

"Well, good." He smiles against my lips. "Now it's time to return the favor. Havin' my cock slidin' between these tits is gonna make me very happy." I come off my elbows and fall back. "Squeeze those tits together for me, Kadence. Squeeze them nice and tight for me." I do as he asks, watching him take some lube from the drawer. He straddles my chest, his erect cock sitting in line with my face. "Lick it, baby." He demands and my mouth listens, opening for my tongue to skirt out between my lips and lick the bead of pre-cum from the tip of his cock.

I look up and lock eyes with him.

"Fuck, Kadence. Don't look fuckin' sexy lickin' my dick or I'll be slidin' it in your mouth instead of between your tits."

"You want my mouth?" I ask, not caring what he wants. I want to make him feel good.

His fingers find my nipples, tweaking and pulling. "No, I need these." He squeezes the lube over his dick, spreading the wetness with a few strokes. I watch him carefully as he lowers his dick to my tits, guiding it in between my breasts. The feeling of his hardness sliding between my softness is not what I was expecting. While the action does nothing to get me off, just watching Nix get lost in the moment does things to my stomach.

"Fuck, babe. Feels so good." His head rolls back and a throb between my legs finds its own beat. I'm so turned on I don't know how much longer I can hold on. He reaches back, finding my aching spot, knowing what I want. *What I need.*

"Jesus, Kadence, you're soaked." He brings his fingers to his mouth tasting me. "Gonna fuckin' feast on you in a minute, baby. But

I want you to come with me first." His fingers find my heat again. My hips buck, needing the release as much as he does.

"You gonna come with me?"

"Yes," I pant as the build up inside of me begins to spiral. The sound of Nix's moans, the pressure of me holding his dick between my breasts and his fingers working my clit is the recipe to finding my release.

"Squeeze me tighter. Milk my cock with those big tits." His dirty talk pulls me further from my mind and closer to my orgasm.

"Nix." My groans turn to begging.

"Look at me. I'll tell you when to come. You hear me?" My eyes fly open and I nod, loving my bossy Nix. "Tell me how much you love me," he commands. His stare holds mine, forcing an answer from me when I struggle to find the words he needs.

"I love you, Nix." The start of my orgasm begins and there's no stopping it.

"Again."

"I love you." Stars spark in my eyes, and my head fills with lust.

"Again."

"I love you, Nix. Love you so much." My body tenses, and the hot flush I've been craving moves through me, heating me, burning me.

"I fuckin' love you, baby."

"Please, Nix," I beg, needing to let go.

"Now, baby." He gives his permission and it only takes a second before we both find our bliss.

"Fuck," he grunts, fucking me over and over, his balls slapping my chest.

"Oh, God!" I cry out, his finger flicking me repeatedly, helping me ride the high of my much-needed orgasm. "Yes, Nix," I squeeze my nipples as I peak, pushing me over the crest. Pleasure and pain courses through me, as his warm cum hits my neck, collarbone and my chest. Coating me. Branding me. Claiming me.

"Baby, that's one of the sexiest things I've ever fuckin' seen," Nix pants after a few beats. Our breathing syncs back to normal and his eyes lock onto his release that I now wear.

"Yeah?" I sigh, still needing a minute to gather myself.

"You wearin' my cum," He shakes his head. "Fuck, I need to claim you more often." He slides out and falls beside me. I release the hold I had on my breasts and drop my hands to my side.

"Claim me all you like, baby. I'm yours."

"Damn straight you are." He rolls over, resting his bent leg over my stomach. "And I'm yours, Kadence. Don't ever fuckin' forget it. You're never gettin' away from me, and if you did try, I'll be here, reclaimin' you all over again."

I don't say anything other than nod.

Nix is my man and nothing will ever come between us.

Coming 2015

Jesse's Story

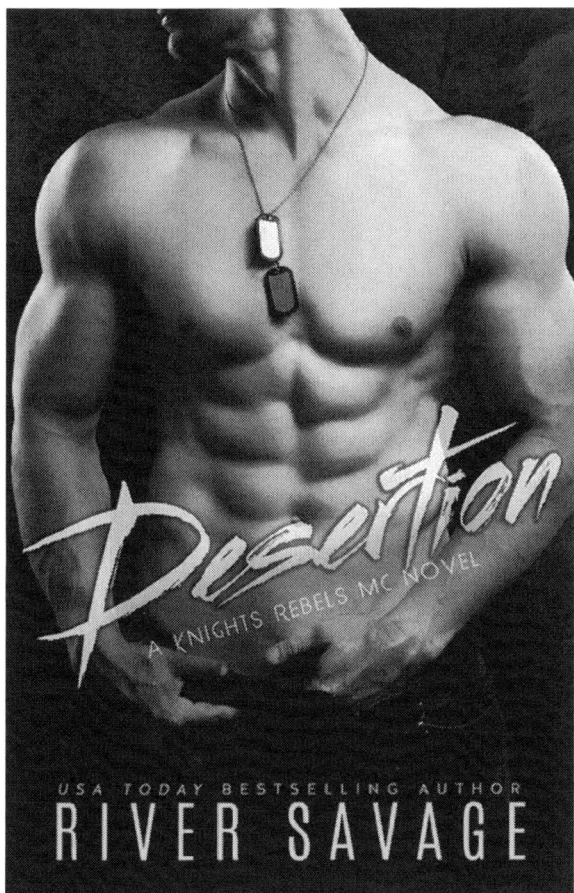

Desertion

A KNIGHTS REBELS MC NOVEL

USA TODAY BESTSELLING AUTHOR

RIVER SAVAGE

Acknowledgments

Alissa Evanson-Smith: *"I'm sorry I can't bring happiness into your world."* I mean those words. I really do love you, soul sister. Rivali. Whore. No other words are needed.

Gillian Grybas: Have I told you I love you? That you are so beautiful? *Reclaimed* is just as much as yours as it is mine. Thank you for your words, for your strength and for being amazing. I can't imagine writing this one without you.

Bel Burgess: You know I need you in my life. I wouldn't survive. Thank you for taking care of my words, for the little encouragements along the way and for just being awesome.

Cassia Brightmore: Dude, I have a girl crush on you. There I said it. Love you, lady. Thank you for your support. It means so much to me.

My beta team: Bel, Brie, Gilly, Jeneane, Nadia, Natalie and Tania. You ladies crack me up. You came in at my time of need. Thank you for your input for Nix and Kadence. I can't wait to work with you all again for Desertion. Love you all.

Louisa from LM Creations: Girl, you know I love you. I love this cover. Once again, you manage to knock it out. Your covers are like a drug. I need more and more.

Becky Johnson: You make my words better. Love you, lady.

Max Henry: You are amazing. Thank you for all that you do for me. I'm so lucky I can call you my friend.

To my Rebels: You know I love you all. I'm so lucky to have you all. #CockOn

To ALL the Bloggers: I wouldn't be able to get my books into readers hands if it wasn't for you. Thank you.

My Mr. Savage: Proof that husbands like Nix do exist. Thank you for all the ups and downs, for the laughs and the tears, for the good and the bad, for when we hit bottom and then we climbed back. I love you. Love isn't a fight, but something worth fighting for.

About the Author

An avid reader of romance and erotic novels, River's love for books and reading fueled her passion for writing. Reading no longer sated her addiction, so she started writing in secret. She never imagined her dream of publishing a novel would ever be achievable. With a soft spot for an alpha male and a snarky, sassy woman, Kadence and Nix were born.

River would love to hear from you. You can contact and/or follow her via...

Email: riversavageauthor@gmail.com
Facebook: https://www.facebook.com/riversavageauthor
Follow River on Twitter: @RiverS_Author

WANT TO KEEP UP TO DATE WITH ALL THE NEWEST NEWS?

Come hang out with River's Rebels

https://www.facebook.com/groups/1513339432229460/

61056079R00058

Made in the USA
Lexington, KY
27 February 2017